Praise for
THE GREAT PET HEIST

SUNSHINE STATE YOUNG READERS AWARD

CHILDREN'S SEQUOYAH BOOK AWARD MASTER LIST

KANSAS NEA READING CIRCLE LIST

BEEHIVE AWARD MASTER LIST

MAINE STUDENT BOOK AWARD READING LIST

HORNED TOAD TALES LIST

MINNESOTA BOOK AWARD NOMINEE

MAGNOLIA BOOK AWARD NOMINEE

"A story sure to charm children who like to imagine
what their beloved pets are up to when they are away."
—*School Library Journal*

"This classic caper may have young readers looking sideways
at their own pets when the story is through."
—*Booklist*

"Bantering dialogue, the distinct personalities of the pets
(expressively illustrated by Mottram), and the whimsical
premise make for an exciting caper."
—*Kirkus Reviews*

THE GREAT VANDAL SCANDAL

Emily Ecton

. . . .

art by *David Mottram*

Atheneum Books for Young Readers
NEW YORK LONDON TORONTO SYDNEY NEW DELHI

ATHENEUM BOOKS FOR YOUNG READERS • An imprint of Simon & Schuster Children's Publishing Division • 1230 Avenue of the Americas, New York, New York 10020 • This book is a work of fiction. Any references to historical events, real people, or real places are used fictitiously. Other names, characters, places, and events are products of the author's imagination, and any resemblance to actual events or places or persons, living or dead, is entirely coincidental. • Text © 2023 by Emily Ecton • Illustration © 2023 by David Mottram • Cover design © 2023 by Simon & Schuster, LLC • All rights reserved, including the right of reproduction in whole or in part in any form. • ATHENEUM BOOKS FOR YOUNG READERS is a registered trademark of Simon & Schuster, LLC. Atheneum logo is a trademark of Simon & Schuster, LLC. • Simon & Schuster: Celebrating 100 Years of Publishing in 2024 • For information about special discounts for bulk purchases, please contact Simon & Schuster Special Sales at 1-866-506-1949 or business@simonandschuster.com. • The Simon & Schuster Speakers Bureau can bring authors to your live event. For more information or to book an event, contact the Simon & Schuster Speakers Bureau at 1-866-248-3049 or visit our website at www.simonspeakers.com. • Also available in an Atheneum Books for Young Readers hardcover edition • The text for this book was set in Adobe Caslon Pro. • The illustrations for this book were rendered digitally. • Manufactured in the United States of America • 0524 MTN • First Atheneum Books for Young Readers paperback edition April 2024 • 10 9 8 7 6 5 4 3 2 • The Library of Congress has cataloged the hardcover edition as follows: • Names: Ecton, Emily, author. | Mottram, Dave, illustrator • Title: The great vandal scandal / Emily Ecton ; art by David Mottram. • Description: First edition. | New York : Atheneum Books for Young Readers, [2023] | Series: The great pet heist ; book 3 | Audience: Ages 8 to 12. • Summary: The animals of the Strathmore building have a mission—convince the raccoons who have invaded the loading dock to leave the building before Biscuit, the Yorkie on the second floor, is evicted for his non-stop barking, and Madison, Butterbean's human, is blamed for the destruction the raccoons are causing. • Identifiers: LCCN 2022006137 | ISBN 9781665919050 (hardcover) | ISBN 9781665919067 (pbk) | ISBN 9781665919074 (ebook) • Subjects: LCSH: Dachshunds—Juvenile fiction. | Yorkshire terrier—Juvenile fiction. | Raccoon—Juvenile fiction. | Animals—Juvenile fiction. | Vandalism—Juvenile fiction. | Humorous stories. | CYAC: Dogs—Fiction. | Pets—Fiction. | Raccoon—Fiction. | Animals—Fiction. | Vandalism—Fiction. | Humorous stories. | LCGFT: Animal fiction. | Humorous fiction. • Classification: LCC PZ7.E21285 Gs 2023 | DDC 813.6 [Fic]—dc23/eng/20220524 • LC record available at https://lccn.loc.gov/2022006137

To my parents.

If anyone deserves this one, it's you.

—E. E.

− 1 −

BUTTERBEAN LIKED TO THINK THAT NOTHING could shock her. She'd been part of an International Crime Syndicate, after all. She was an experienced Ghost Investigator. But this? Nothing had prepared her for this.

Mrs. Food had been eating tuna fish for the past five minutes and hadn't offered her a bite once. NOT EVEN ONCE.

Butterbean scooted forward until her chin was practically in Mrs. Food's lap. Maybe Mrs. Food just hadn't seen her. That was the only logical explanation.

"You're not getting any, Bean," Mrs. Food said, her mouth full. "Stop begging."

Butterbean fell backward in shock. BEGGING? As if a Ghost Investigator would resort to BEGGING. She was simply making herself available. Staying open to opportunities. And if that opportunity happened to be a mouthful of tuna fish, so be it.

Walt stopped licking her paw and looked over at the crumpled pile of what used to be Butterbean. "Do I even want to know?" she asked Oscar.

Oscar opened his beak to answer and then reconsidered. He shook his head. "No."

"For the record, I was NOT begging," Butterbean grumbled, picking herself up and stomping over to the living room. "I was very restrained."

"It's true!" Polo called from the rat cage. "I saw the whole thing!"

"Me too," Marco said, climbing up onto the water bottle. "Oooh, you know what this calls for? I think this calls for an investigation!"

"Yes!" Polo narrowed her eyes. "Why wouldn't Mrs. Food give Butterbean any of her tuna fish? Very suspicious, if you ask me. Mysterious, even."

"Yeah! Mysterious!" Marco agreed. "We should definitely investigate."

Oscar groaned. There hadn't been much to investigate since they'd solved the mysterious haunting of Apartment 5B, it was true. But that didn't mean the rats hadn't tried. There had been the mysterious case of Madison's missing hairbrush. (It fell behind the bed.) Mrs. Food's suspicious behavior involving a series of mysterious and very short phone calls. (Telemarketer.) And the mysterious disappearance of Walt's favorite seafood treats. (Chad ate them. He was an octopus they knew who lived on the eighth floor. And to be honest, he was usually behind any mysterious food disappearances.) Oscar was beginning to think that the rats didn't really understand the meaning of the word "mysterious."

"That's not a mystery," Oscar said. "We've talked about this."

"Are we sure, though?" Polo asked. "Seems kind of mysterious to me."

"Maybe we should investigate why it isn't mysterious," Marco said thoughtfully.

"Maybe we should investigate why you want to investigate everything," Walt said, resuming her paw licking. "Begging isn't allowed. Mystery solved."

"I WAS NOT BEGGING!" Butterbean barked. "I WAS WATCHING CLOSELY."

Walt rolled her eyes. "Fine. Watching closely is also not allowed. Not at mealtimes."

"Well, when you put it that way," Marco said. Walt was an amazing investigator.

"You know," Oscar said thoughtfully. "Since there aren't any crimes going on, I think it might be time for us to officially retire."

"Retire?" Marco gasped. "You mean *retire* retire?" As far as he was concerned, being an investigator was the best thing that had ever happened to him. Well, that and being part of an International Crime Syndicate. Not many rats had that kind of résumé.

"Can you even retire from being an investigator?" Polo asked.

"I think we can," Oscar said. "Besides, we have lots of other things to do now. I, for one, am thinking of improving my Human language skills. How does this sound?" He cleared his throat. *"Quiet, Oscar!"* He looked around expectantly. "That was me being Mrs. Food, in case you couldn't tell."

"I could tell," Butterbean said. She'd heard Mrs. Food say that a lot.

Walt raised one eyebrow. "Impressive."

Polo shot Marco a look. "Um, yeah. It sounded just like her."

"Like looking in a mirror!" Marco piped up. "Or, no. I mean . . ."

"OOOHHH! Do the elevator lady voice next!" Butterbean said, wagging her tail. She loved the voice in the elevator that told you what floor you were on.

"It's just a little something I've been working on," Oscar said, preening. "I still need more practice."

"What needs more practice?" Wallace, a wild rat who used to live in the vents, peeked around the edge of the sofa to make sure it was all clear.

"We're talking about retiring from the investigating business," Polo explained. "We've all got lots of other things to do. Oscar is going to work on his Human language skills."

"Yeah," Marco said. "And me and Polo, we're, um . . ." He hesitated, looking around the cage. "Well, these seeds aren't going to sort themselves," he said, staring at the scattered seeds doubtfully.

"And I'm going to be a therapist!" Butterbean said.

Everyone stared at her.

Wallace shot a look at Polo, who shrugged. "Um, sure, okay," Wallace said finally. "Well, I'm super busy too. I finally moved out of Apartment 5B and set up my sleeping bag behind the couch in 7C." Wallace had used one of Madison's pom-pom socks as a sleeping bag during a stakeout once, and he may have forgotten to give it back. It was one of his prized possessions.

"Wait, 7C? Mrs. Power Walker's apartment? Are you moving there for sure?" Butterbean asked. Mrs. Power Walker was one of Butterbean's favorite residents in the

Strathmore Building. She was always really friendly in the elevator, pushing buttons when needed and never asking questions. The perfect neighbor.

Wallace shrugged. "I'm not ready to move my collection of lost keys in or anything, but it looks promising. She leaves a bowl of milk out every night, so that's a plus. She says it's for the brownies. I think that's a kind of fairy," Wallace explained.

"No, brownies are like cookies but fatter," Butterbean said. "Like flat cake."

"That's true," Polo agreed. "Madison eats them."

Oscar closed his eyes. He decided not to say anything.

"Well, I haven't seen any, so I think it's fair game," Wallace said. "I'm not turning down free milk."

"Sure," Butterbean said. Free milk was free milk.

"See? It sounds like we won't even miss being investigators," Oscar said, clicking his beak. "What with Wallace's new apartment, Marco and Polo with their seed sorting, Walt with her . . ."

"Relaxing," Walt said. "I'm planning on doing some high-quality relaxing."

"Right. Relaxing. And Butterbean with her—"

"Being a therapist," Butterbean said, nodding.

"Um. Right," Oscar finished lamely. He didn't even want to ask. But somebody had to. "Butterbean, about this therapist job—"

"You can't just decide to be a therapist," Walt interrupted.

Butterbean looked offended. "I'm not. It's a real job."

Walt sighed. "Of course it is, but you're a wiener dog. Do you really think—"

She hadn't even finished the sentence when the front door slammed open, and Madison Park, the medium-sized girl who lived with them, rushed into the room waving a piece of paper over her head.

"It's all set!" she said, dropping her backpack and throwing herself into the chair next to Mrs. Food.

"Well, hello to you too," Mrs. Food said, swallowing the last of her tuna. Butterbean looked mournfully at the empty plate. It was so unfair.

"Right, sorry, hello. But it's all set! See?" She pushed the piece of paper toward Mrs. Food. "I got the appointment for Butterbean."

Mrs. Food peered down at the paper through her glasses. "Well, isn't that something!"

Madison jumped up and hurried over to Butterbean. "You're going to be great, Bean!" She kissed Butterbean on the head. "She's going to be perfect. Look at her—she even looks like a therapy dog!" Madison rubbed Butterbean's ears and then rushed off toward her bedroom. "I can't wait to e-mail Aunt Ruby!" Madison was staying with Mrs. Food while her aunt was deployed overseas.

7

"Therapy dog?" Oscar said slowly. It was all making sense now.

"I told you. I'm going to be a therapist," Butterbean said smugly.

Walt raised an eyebrow. "I don't think it's quite the same thing, Bean."

"You're just jealous because I'm going to have my own practice," Butterbean said.

"OOOOoooh, are we talking about our careers? Me next, please."

Everyone jumped at the voice. (Marco hit his head on the bottom of the water bottle.) "DON'T DO THAT!" Marco said, rubbing his head.

"Sorry, did I scare you?" The white cat emerged

from behind the couch and blinked at them innocently. "Oops. My bad."

"YOU KNOW YOU DID!" Polo said. "And you can't just come in like that. Mrs. Food is RIGHT THERE!" She waved her arms in the direction of the dining room table.

"Relax, you know I always keep out of sight," the white cat said. She lived on the fifth floor but didn't see anything wrong with using the vents to explore other apartments. "So did I tell you I've come out of retirement?" The white cat was the cat featured in all the Beautiful Buffet Cat Food commercials. (Print and television.)

"Only a million times," Marco grumbled softly.

"Sales of Beautiful Buffet Cat Food PLUM-METED when I retired. They practically begged me to come back. I didn't have the heart to say no." The white cat curled her tail around her feet.

"So you've said," Oscar said politely. He'd heard the story so many times he could practically recite it word for word.

"Well, it's true," the white cat said.

"I've got a career now too," Butterbean said. "I'm going to be a therapist. That's why we're all retiring from investigating, because we've got so much to do."

"Hmm. Well, good to know. Of course, that's bad

news for Biscuit, but I guess he'll figure things out himself." The white cat lashed her tail in the air as she turned to go back behind the couch.

"Wait, Biscuit? What's wrong with Biscuit?" Butterbean asked, frowning.

"Oh, nothing important." The white cat waved a paw dismissively. "Nothing that a career dog like you should worry about."

"But which Biscuit?" Butterbean asked. There were a lot of Biscuits in the building, and Butterbean was friends with them all. "Second Floor Biscuit? Eighth Floor Biscuit? Biscuit with the Slobber Problem? Biscuit who—"

"Second Floor," the white cat said. "But like I said, he'll probably be fine. I'm sure he'll survive somehow." She turned to leave, but Walt blocked her path.

"Okay, spill it." Walt's whiskers were bristling. She didn't have strong feelings about any of the Biscuits, but she didn't love the way the white cat was toying with them. "What's wrong with Second Floor Biscuit?"

"Well, if you must know," the white cat said, her eyes gleaming. "Your friend is in big trouble." She made a sympathetic face at Butterbean. "He's getting evicted. Kicked out. By this time next week, your little friend will be out on the street."

– 2 –

"WELL, THAT WAS FUN," BUTTERBEAN SAID, getting up. "Retirement is over. Time to investigate."

Oscar hopped onto the side of his cage. "What? But we just agreed!" He had really hoped to be retired for more than five minutes.

Walt put a paw on Butterbean's back. "Butterbean, calm down. We don't even know if there's anything to investigate at this point." She turned to the white cat. "We need details. Why is Second Floor Biscuit getting kicked out?"

The white cat stood up, stretched, and then sat back down. "Well—"

"So wait, Second Floor Biscuit, he's the one with

the good haircut?" Polo interrupted. She had seen him once when she was out with Butterbean. He was a pretty fashionable dog.

Butterbean cringed. "Well, not anymore," she said slowly. She leaned forward. "There was a grooming incident," she whispered, spraying Polo with a fine mist of spit. "He's got bangs now." She nodded significantly. "I mean . . . BANGS."

"Oooohhhhh," Polo said, her eyes widening. "But . . ." She hesitated. "Bangs aren't bad, are they?" She'd seen lots of people with bangs. Fashionable people, even.

"Not usually. But these?" Butterbean made a face. "Trust me. They're bad."

"Okay, wow," Polo said. "Bad bangs." She smoothed down her own fur in sympathy.

"SERIOUSLY?" Marco stomped over, rolling his eyes so much it was surprising he could stand upright. "You guys are talking about BANGS? Who cares about a dumb hairdo? We need to know what's wrong with Biscuit! I'm pretty sure it's not BANGS!" He waved his paws at the white cat. "You! Explain!"

"Barking. It's a barking problem," the white cat said, smirking. "Nonstop, from what I hear. Nobody knows why, and the humans are MAD."

"Bangs," Butterbean said knowingly.

"Doubtful," Walt said.

"It's probably not the bangs, Bean," Oscar said. "Marco's right. No one barks that much over a haircut. Hair does grow out, after all."

"Besides, haircut emergencies are more a cry-in-the-corner kind of situation," Walt said. Not that she'd ever had a haircut. She looked around. "Right?"

Marco and Polo shrugged. They'd never had haircuts either.

"It does seem mysterious," Polo said. "For real this time."

"Not like the tuna fish," Marco added. "Sorry, Butterbean."

Butterbean nodded. It was definitely more mysterious than the tuna fish.

Oscar cocked his head. "I have to admit, it does seem strange. But I don't see that there's anything we can do. Shouldn't he just stop barking?"

"Well, duh," the white cat said, getting up. "That's pretty obvious. But he won't."

"Then I don't know what to say," Oscar said. "I'm sorry, Butterbean. Even if we weren't retired from investigating, I don't see how we could help."

"But if I could just talk to him . . ." Butterbean whimpered. "I could therapy him!"

Walt sighed. "Sure. Maybe. But you can't do

anything tonight. Whatever we do will have to wait until tomorrow."

"If he lasts that long," the white cat snorted. "Sorry to say it, but that dog is toast."

"WHAT?" Butterbean yelped. "OSCAR!"

"Um, how about us?" Polo interrupted, tentatively raising a paw. "We could check. If you want."

"We can't do therapy like Butterbean—" Marco said.

"But we can go in the vents. We could tell Biscuit to keep quiet until tomorrow," Polo said.

"Really?" Butterbean sniffled.

"I mean, the seed sorting can probably wait a little longer," Marco said.

"The seeds aren't actually that important," Polo agreed.

"Would that make you feel better, Butterbean?" Oscar asked, watching Butterbean carefully. She was twitching like she might start doing laps around the room, and nobody wanted that.

"And it's not like we'd be INVESTIGATING," Polo said carefully. "Since we're retired. We'll just be CHECKING IN."

"Yeah, passing a message," Marco said. His whiskers trembled as he looked at Polo. "A SECRET message."

Polo clutched at Marco's arm. "LIKE SPIES!" Polo

squealed. "WE CAN BE A SECRET SPY ORGA-NIZATION." She turned to Oscar, her eyes shining.

Oscar groaned.

"OOOHHH, CAN I BE A SPY TOO?" Butterbean yelped eagerly. "I'll be a THERAPIST SPY."

"I don't think therapists are supposed to be spies," Oscar said doubtfully.

"But don't you see? That's why it's perfect! NO ONE WILL SUSPECT ME!" Butterbean was practically levitating, she was bouncing up and down so fast.

Oscar had to admit, a Secret Spy Organization did sound pretty exciting. And he didn't know any other mynah birds who were International Crime Bosses, Ghost Investigators, AND Secret Spies. He would be the first. It was an appealing idea.

Oscar nodded. "Okay, we'll see how the secret messaging goes first. Then we can decide on the Secret Spy Organization."

"YAY! We're SPIES!" Polo cheered, high-fiving Marco as they climbed out of their cage.

"WHOOHOO SPIES!" Marco and Polo edged past the white cat into the opening of the vent. "Excuse me, white cat. You didn't see a thing. Because we're STEALTHY SPIES."

"I don't believe this." The white cat shook her head as the rats streaked past her.

Their voices echoed as they disappeared into the vents. "SECRET SPY MISSION—GO!"

If Marco and Polo had had any doubts about the white cat's story, they went away pretty quickly. Because the white cat was right—there was no ignoring that barking.

"It's not so much that it's loud," Polo said thoughtfully as they slid down a vent. "It's more . . . piercing."

"Like if a car alarm was a dog," Marco agreed. He didn't personally own a car, but he'd seen car alarms on TV, and he always had to cover his ears.

"Exactly," Polo said.

"I can see why Bob is upset," Marco said, following the yips. Although, to be fair, it didn't take a lot to make Bob upset. Bob was the maintenance man in the building, and just catching a glimpse of Marco and Polo in the vent opening one time had made him rip the grate cover off with his bare hands. Marco still had nightmares about that sometimes.

By the time they made it to the second-floor vents, the barking had reached hands-over-ears levels. Polo pointed to a grate at the end of the vent. "That one."

Marco nodded and took a step toward it. Then he hesitated. "So we use our spy skills to pass Biscuit our message, and then we get out. No hair commentary, okay?" He still couldn't believe they'd wasted so much time earlier talking about hairdos.

"Okay." Polo nodded. It's not like she hadn't seen bad hair before. After all, she'd seen Butterbean in the morning. "We'll be fast. No bangs talk."

She and Marco fist-bumped and then peeked into the room.

The lights in Biscuit's apartment were mostly off, but they could tell that the living room was a lot like Mrs. Food's, with cozy-looking furniture and doilies on the tables. It was totally empty, except for one small figure silhouetted in the window. A Yorkshire terrier–shaped figure. Biscuit.

He was standing on a cushioned bench in the shadows, and he was obviously very angry. He was barking so furiously that every bark lifted him off his feet. His face was so close to the window that he'd smeared the glass with an elaborate design using only the moisture from his nose. (Polo was pretty sure that part was unintentional.)

"There he is. YOOHOO! BISCUIT!" Polo leaned forward to get a closer look.

It was only then that Biscuit stepped out of the shadows.

Polo blinked. Twice.

"Whoa!" Polo staggered back in shock. "Wow. I

mean. Um. I think that's Biscuit." She composed herself just in time. They had a plan, and the plan didn't involve hair commentary.

Polo took a deep breath and waved her arm. "Um, MR. BISCUIT!" she called. "UP HERE!"

She had almost caught Biscuit's eye when she heard a gasp next to her.

"HOLY COW." Marco grabbed Polo's free arm. "POLO! Polo, holy cow. Look at those BANGS!"

"Focus on the assignment! Remember? No hair commentary?" Polo hissed.

Spies didn't get distracted by bad bangs (even if they really wanted to).

"But those are PEOPLE BANGS!" Marco pressed his face against the grate to get a better look. "That dog has PEOPLE BANGS."

Polo nodded grimly. Biscuit's hair had been lopped off just above the eyes, giving him thick, heavy bangs that made him look like he had a human bowl-cut hairdo.

Marco couldn't help but stare. Maybe Butterbean was right about the barking. Those bangs would make him angry too.

"Don't look at the bangs," Polo said. "Just look at something else."

"Right, right," Marco said, taking a deep breath and looking away from the bangs. "We're professionals,

I know. We're spies. We can't get distracted. It's just . . . wait, what's with his FEET?"

The bangs were bad enough. Polo didn't want to look at the feet. But there was no way she could resist. She looked at the feet.

Polo gave a shrill squeak and stopped waving.

Biscuit's hair was still long and luxurious, just like it had been when she'd seen him before. But it had been cut straight across about three inches from the floor, so Biscuit's shaved naked feet stuck out awkwardly. It looked like he was wearing a silky horse blanket. Or a caftan. Or some kind of grass skirt. It was like the whole haircut was designed to draw attention to his tiny naked feet.

"Butterbean told us it was bad," Polo said.

"I know." Naked dog feet weren't something Marco thought should bother him, but for some reason they really did.

Polo snapped out of it first. She put her hands on Marco's shoulders. "We need to pull ourselves together! Forget the feet. Forget the bangs. We're SECRET SPIES. We need to pass on our message."

Marco nodded. "You're right." He stepped forward and hissed through the grate. "BISCUIT!"

Biscuit's ears swiveled around as he scanned the room. "SHOW YOURSELVES, INTRUDERS!" he barked angrily. "YOU'RE NO MATCH FOR ME! I'LL STOP YOU! YOU'LL NEVER TAKE THIS APARTMENT!"

Polo glanced anxiously at Marco. That wasn't exactly the reception she'd expected. She stuck her arm out of the vent again and waved in what she hoped was a cheery spy-message kind of way.

"Um, Biscuit, hi," Polo yelled. "Calm down! We're friends! We're here with a message."

"I'LL RIP YOU TO SHREDS!" Biscuit barked. "I'LL TAKE YOU APART!"

"Right. So, um, we've got a message from Butter-bean," Marco called.

"She's coming to help!" Polo added. "We're here

to help!" It was hard to keep waving enthusiastically while Biscuit was threatening them like that. "But you need to stop barking!"

"I'LL RIP YOUR EARS OFF!" Biscuit barked so hard that he fell off the bench, then growled and turned on it like the bench had personally attacked him. "I'LL USE YOUR TAILS FOR DENTAL FLOSS!"

"Goodness," Polo said, thrown. She hadn't expected Biscuit to be quite so descriptive.

Marco touched his tail carefully. "Can he do that?" he whispered. "The tail thing?" He was kind of attached to his tail.

Polo shook her head. "He's bluffing," she said. She just hoped she was right.

She took a deep breath and tried again. "We know Butterbean, your friend. She will—"

"So you've got Butterbean, have you?" Biscuit growled. "WELL, YOU WON'T GET PAST ME!" He let off another volley of barking, leaping on and off the bench and racing around the room.

A loud thumping sound came from the apartment next door. "QUIET!" a voice shouted.

Biscuit turned to the wall and let out a howl.

"That must be Teacher Man," Polo said. "In 2B?"

"We should go. We're making it worse," Marco said,

watching Biscuit race around the room. He'd never heard Teacher Man yell like that. "But we did what we said we'd do. We passed on the message. So it was kind of a successful mission?"

"I guess," Polo said. They hadn't been very successful at getting Biscuit to stop barking.

Marco backed away from the grate. "I don't think we convinced him, though."

Polo shook her head. "No. But did you see? He was looking out of that window. He's barking at something specific." The fur on her neck prickled. "Something outside."

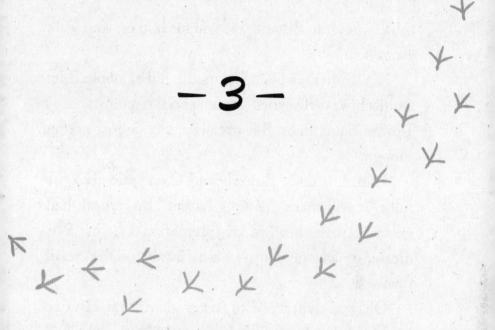

– 3 –

"So the first thing we need to do," Oscar said, watching Mrs. Food carefully, "is to come up with a plan."

Mrs. Food and Madison were in the dining room having breakfast. Oscar usually had his breakfast then too, but these were special circumstances. If the white cat was right, they didn't have much time. His stomach would have to wait.

"Right," Walt agreed. (She'd had her breakfast earlier.) "We need to figure out how Butterbean can make contact. Once we've done that, we can set up the meeting."

Oscar cocked his head. "Butterbean, where do you

usually run into Biscuit? Do you see him on your walk every day?"

"No," Butterbean said, her mouth full of kibble. (Her stomach wasn't worried about special circumstances.) "I mean, sometimes. But not always. It doesn't matter, though."

"I think it does, Butterbean," Oscar said thoughtfully. "It will make planning harder." Butterbean had never been the head of an International Crime Syndicate, so she obviously wasn't aware of the detail involved.

"Oh, you don't need to worry about that," Butterbean said, drooling a little as she finished the kibble. "I have a plan already. It's all set."

Oscar blinked.

"You have a plan," he said.

"Yup," Butterbean said.

"It's all set," Oscar said.

"Yup," Butterbean said, licking her food dish. "I worked it out with Marco and Polo. We've got it all figured out."

"You worked it out. With Marco and Polo?" Oscar looked at the rats questioningly.

"We're STEALTHY SPIES now, Oscar!" Polo said proudly. "We came up with a SUPER-SECRET PLAN."

Marco nodded, doing some stretches. It was important to warm up before a super-secret spy mission. "We thought since it was our first mission—"

"Second mission," Polo interrupted.

"Second mission," Marco corrected himself. "We thought we should keep it simple. We could use extra help, though."

"Are you in?" Polo asked, bobbing anxiously on the balls of her feet. "We need you, Oscar."

"You too, Walt," Marco said, doing air punches as he ran in place. "We need all the help we can get."

"Trust us—it's a solid plan," Polo said. "It's pretty much guaranteed to succeed."

"Pretty much," Marco agreed.

Walt shrugged. "We're in," she said. There was no point in arguing, not with those kind of odds. "Pretty much guaranteed success, Oscar," she said with a raised eyebrow.

"So you're, what, just hoping that you'll run into Biscuit on your walk?" Oscar didn't think that sounded like pretty much guaranteed success, especially given how easily Butterbean was distracted. It sounded like pretty much guaranteed failure.

"No," Butterbean snorted. "Don't be silly. I wouldn't do that."

"Well, good, because—"

Butterbean sat up straighter. "I'm going to his apartment."

Oscar stared at her. "You're just . . . going to his apartment?" Well, it was a simple plan, he had to give them that much.

"Wait, what?" Walt tried to keep her expression neutral.

"Isn't that perfect? We've got it all worked out," Polo said.

"But you can't fit in the vents," Walt said slowly.

"We're not using them," Marco said. "Butterbean's just taking a little detour on her walk. That's all."

Walt and Oscar exchanged a look. Oscar sighed. "Okay. Sure. What do we do?" He could already think of a million ways this could go wrong, but he wasn't going to say anything. They weren't supposed to be investigating things anyway. They were supposed to be retired.

"Okay, I'll fill you in on the TOP SECRET PLANS," Butterbean said, spraying a fine mist of kibble dust as she hurried over to Oscar's cage. When she got there, she looked around carefully before leaning against the cage stand in her most casual way. She didn't want to be too obvious.

"So this is the plan," Butterbean whispered once she was sure no one was watching them. "When Mrs. Food and Madison finish breakfast, we're going to—"

"Okay, Bean!" Madison called, getting up from the table and picking up Butterbean's leash. "Come on. Time for your walk!"

Butterbean's eyes got wide. "OH NO. OSCAR! OH NO!" She jumped to her feet, bumping Oscar's cage and making it sway dangerously from side to side. Oscar clung to his perch. When he'd thought of a million ways that things could go wrong, he hadn't thought of that.

Butterbean lolled her tongue out of her mouth as she trotted over to Madison. "You'll know what to do. Just wait for the signal!" she called over her shoulder.

"Just follow our lead, okay, Oscar?" Polo shouted as she ran to the far end of the cage. "POSITIONS, EVERY-BODY! Your position is, um, your cage, I guess, Oscar."

Oscar got in position, which was pretty much the same place he'd been standing before.

"Don't worry, Butterbean!" Marco yelled, as he took his position at the other end of the cage. "We've got you covered!"

Madison clipped the leash onto Butterbean's collar. "Ready to go? We can't waste time today. I don't want to be late." Even though Madison was living with Mrs. Food while her aunt was overseas, she still had to do regular human things like go to school.

Butterbean threw a significant look over her shoulder at Marco and Polo as she trotted behind Madison to the front door. She stood perfectly still as Madison put on her jacket and unlocked the door. But as soon as the door opened, she gave a low bark. "NOW!"

Marco and Polo sprang into action. Marco immediately started jumping as high as he could, so that he hit the lid of the cage. (He was particularly good at hitting it so that it made a hollow WHOOMP noise.) Polo's specialty was doing running kicks at the water bottle, so that it clattered against the glass. It was pretty effective. The aquarium was vibrating so much, it looked like it might fall off the table.

"What the heck?" Madison said, looking back at the rat cage. "You guys! What are you doing?"

Oscar nodded to himself. "Distraction . . . I see.

I can do distraction." It wasn't his usual assignment, but he was more than able to improvise. With a loud squawk he leaped from his perch and fluttered against the bars of his cage, making it sway back and forth.

"WHAT THE HECK?" Madison's eyes grew wide. "OSCAR?"

Mrs. Food came out of the kitchen, wiping her hands on a dish towel. "What in the world?"

Madison dropped Butterbean's leash and let go of the door as she hurried toward the animal cages. That was all the opening Butterbean needed. Taking a deep breath (and scooping up her leash in her mouth), Butterbean made a dash for it, slipping out of the door just as it swung shut. She was in the hallway before Madison even realized what was happening.

But she wasn't alone. Walt was right behind her.

"Walt? You're coming too?" Butterbean gasped as she raced for the elevator.

"Think of me as insurance," Walt said.

Butterbean jumped up to hit the call button for the elevator, keeping one eye on Mrs. Food's door at the end of the hall. She had to make it into the elevator before Madison noticed she was gone, or the whole plan would fall apart. And the elevator was slower than ever.

Walt sat and watched the numbers over the elevator. "So what happens if Madison comes out before the elevator gets here? Do you have a contingency plan?"

"Improvise," Butterbean said. She'd seen a show about improvising once, and it seemed like a fancy way of making stuff up. She was good at making stuff up. Or at least she hoped she was.

The apartment door opened a crack. They could hear the ruckus inside. It looked like they were out of time.

Butterbean set her jaw. Time to improvise. She stood up. Not that she knew what she was going to do, that is. But standing up seemed to be an important first step.

But just as she did, the elevator dinged and the doors opened.

"RUN!" Butterbean yelled, dashing inside with Walt

close behind. She jumped up, hitting the button for the second floor, and pawed at the close doors button. The doors started to close. Butterbean slumped against the wall. They'd made it.

The doors were almost completely shut when an arm shot into the elevator between them, making them bounce open again.

"HA!" Madison said, pushing her way inside. "Not so fast, you weird dog." She bent down and picked up Butterbean's leash. "What is wrong with you all today? You're not going for a solo walk, Butterbean. Sheesh." She leaned against the back of the elevator.

"So your plan is to just run out of the elevator?" Walt asked from her location behind Madison. She didn't think she'd been spotted yet.

"When I get to the second floor, yeah, pretty much," Butterbean said under her breath. She watched the numbers. Madison being in the elevator was not part of the plan, but she wasn't giving up. Not yet.

"Second floor," the elevator voice said. Butterbean leaned forward, her muscles tensed and ready.

The doors opened. Butterbean could hear Biscuit's barks echoing from down the hall.

Butterbean sprang forward. And immediately flopped back as she reached the end of the leash. She didn't even make it out of the elevator.

Madison shook her head and gave her a grim smile. "Nice try, dog," she said. She had the leash in a tight grip and was holding it extra close. Madison had thought of everything.

"Well, shoot," Butterbean said, standing up. The doors closed again. She was out of ideas. The next stop was the lobby. She didn't know how to get back to the second floor once they got to the lobby.

"Ahem." Walt stepped out of the shadowy corner and winked at Butterbean. "See? Insurance," she said, sitting down and licking her paw.

Madison gasped. "Walt? You got out too?"

"Lobby," the elevator voice said as the doors opened.

Madison blocked the exit. "Sorry, Bean, we've got to go back. We can't go out until we take Walt back." Madison hit the button for the fourth floor and then leaned down awkwardly to hold on to Walt to keep her from running away. "Stay here, Walt."

She glanced at her watch. The last thing she needed was a tardy.

"Are you addressing me?"

Madison looked over her shoulder into the lobby and turned red. A middle-aged woman was staring at the three of them with a pinched expression. "Oh, I-I'm sorry," Madison stammered. "I just—"

"Yes, I can see," the woman said. "Quite the zoo. Thank you, but I'd prefer to wait." She frowned at Butterbean with distaste.

Butterbean glared back. "Mrs. Hates Dogs on Six," she muttered under her breath. They had a history.

"Thanks, I'm sorry, they just . . ." Madison said apologetically before trailing off and staring down at Walt. Mrs. Hates Dogs on Six raised an eyebrow.

Butterbean stared stonily at Mrs. Hates Dogs on Six until the doors started to close. Then she jumped up and hit the button for the second floor. She looked over at Walt. "Ready?"

"Ready," Walt said.

"Second floor," the elevator voice said.

The doors opened.

Walt and Butterbean both made a dash for the doors. Butterbean's hind feet were moving so fast that they almost passed her front feet. The leash jerked, catching Madison by surprise this time and yanking her forward. The leash flew out of her hand.

"BUTTERBEAN!" Madison squealed as she hurried after them. This was not the way she had planned to spend her morning.

"BISCUIT! BISCUIT!" Butterbean yelled as she raced to Biscuit's door and threw herself against it, clawing at the handle. "OPEN UP!"

It wouldn't budge. "WHY DO PEOPLE LOCK THEIR DOORS!" Butterbean wailed as she tried again. "I CAN'T GET IN!"

Walt jumped up and rang the doorbell as she looked behind them. Madison had almost caught up. "Talk fast, Bean, we only have a second."

"BISCUIT, IT'S BUTTERBEAN," Butterbean barked through the door. "YOU NEED TO—"

She stopped abruptly. Because the front door had been thrown open.

In the doorway stood Biscuit's human, Mrs. Biscuit.

"Um," Butterbean said. She didn't know what to say to Mrs. Biscuit. They'd never officially met.

"Um," Mrs. Biscuit said, looking down at the dog and cat standing at her feet.

"Um," Madison said, racing up behind them and looking back and forth between Mrs. Biscuit and Butterbean and Walt. This was pretty bad. She was definitely going to get in trouble for this.

Biscuit stuck his head out from behind Mrs. Biscuit's legs. He had a wild look around the eyes, like he hadn't slept at all. He stared at Butterbean in confusion. "Butterbean?"

"Biscuit, we need to talk," Butterbean said. "Excuse me." She pushed past Mrs. Biscuit's legs and squeezed into the apartment. Walt slipped in on the other side.

Mrs. Biscuit blinked at Madison, who blinked
back. "Um, hi?" Madison said after a long second.
"So . . . I guess my dog wants to play with your dog?"
She was definitely going to be late.

– 4 –

"PLEASE, HAVE A SEAT," MRS. BISCUIT SAID to Madison, waving vaguely at the sofa. "I think this is the first time he's stopped barking in days."

Madison sat on the very edge of the sofa and tried not to look at her watch. She was not going to be here long, not if she could help it. And technically, she was in charge, not Butterbean. She didn't know why it didn't feel that way.

"So he's been barking a lot, then?" Madison said, trying to be polite. She'd seen him around, of course, but she didn't even know this dog. Not really.

"Nonstop," Mrs. Biscuit said grimly, watching Butterbean and Biscuit sniff each other. She flashed a tight smile at Madison. Madison gave a weak smile back.

Walt kept an eye on Madison as she turned to Biscuit. "Okay, quick. We don't have much time," Walt said. "Spill it, dog. What's the situation?"

"I don't know what you mean," Biscuit said gruffly. "There's no situation. I've got everything under control." He blew air out of his nose loudly.

"Give me a break," Walt said.

"Walt, let me handle this. Biscuit, that's not what we heard," Butterbean said softly, in her best therapist voice. "I tried to get a message to you last night. Word on the street is that you're about to get kicked out for barking. How does that make you feel?"

"What message? Last night?" Biscuit looked suspicious. "I didn't get any message."

Butterbean frowned. Maybe it would've worked better if she'd had Biscuit lie down on the couch. That seemed to be the prime therapy position, at least from what she'd seen on the Television. She tried again. "The white cat said you were in trouble, so we sent Marco and Polo to tell you we were coming. They were in the vents."

"Marco and Polo are rats," Walt added.

"So those things in the vents were your friends? Well, thanks for the extra trauma, I guess," Biscuit said grouchily.

"We just wanted to help." Butterbean tried to keep her voice even. Being a therapist was harder than she'd expected.

"Look, I've got enough invaders to deal with, okay? I don't need any extras from you. I'm already having to monitor the perimeter of the apartment 24-7."

"Invaders? What invaders?" Butterbean frowned. "Where?"

On the couch, Madison clasped her hands together and leaned forward. "So!"

"Uh-oh," Walt said.

"You know, we should really get out of your hair," Madison said, smiling. She could probably still make it on time, if she brushed her teeth really quickly. That would do it. She'd just be super fast. "This was a lot of fun, though."

"Oh no, please. Give them just a few more minutes. They're being so quiet," Mrs. Biscuit said, gripping Madison by the arm a little too tightly. She had a strange hollow look around her eyes too, just like Biscuit. "There's been so much barking."

"But . . ." Madison looked over at the pets, who had frozen and were watching her carefully. She shrugged and sank back down onto the couch. "Okay, I guess. Just a few minutes." She didn't really need to brush her teeth.

Mrs. Biscuit gave her a weak smile.

Walt lashed her tail in the air. "Come on, Biscuit. We're on a deadline."

"If the white cat knows the situation, it's all over the building. So you might as well share. Express your emotions. Um. Find your center." Butterbean wished she knew more therapy terms, but she hadn't even started her classes yet.

Biscuit snorted. "Look, that's not my problem. My problem is—"

Mrs. Biscuit sneezed softly.

"Excuse me. INSPECTION!" Biscuit yelled, launching himself up into Mrs. Biscuit's lap. He examined her nose thoroughly, and after a few seconds, he nodded in satisfaction. "Okay, all clear."

"Um," Madison said.

"That's just something he does," Mrs. Biscuit said, dabbing her nose with a tissue.

Biscuit jumped off the couch. "Sorry, just one of my dogly duties."

"Wait, what? Sneeze inspections are a DOGLY DUTY?" Butterbean had never once inspected Mrs. Food's nose after a sneeze.

"It's not a requirement, Bean," Walt said softly. She really didn't want sneeze inspections to become a thing.

"But if it's a DUTY—" Butterbean started.

"My PROBLEM, since you're so concerned," interrupted Biscuit as he trotted over, "is the INVADERS on the LOADING DOCK!" He jumped up onto the cushioned bench under the window. Butterbean's eyes widened. It was like his feet were made of springs.

Biscuit pressed his face close to the glass, making more nose smears. Butterbean was surprised he could even see outside anymore.

"Oh no, here we go," Mrs. Biscuit said, holding her breath.

"Invaders? That's your problem?" Walt jumped up onto the bench and looked out of the window. "Oh come on, Biscuit. Seriously?"

"What?" Butterbean said, jumping up clumsily after

them. She didn't want to miss out on any invaders. Maybe she could do some therapy on them.

Walt rolled her eyes. "That's the loading dock. Those invaders? They're the loading dock rats. Are you seriously freaked out because of a couple of rats?"

"Our friend Wallace knows the loading dock rats," Butterbean said, finally getting her footing. That bench was taller than it looked. "They're not bad. Did you just notice them or something? Because I think they've always lived there."

Biscuit made a face. "No, the loading dock rats aren't freaking me out. I've lived here my whole life—you think I care about a couple of rats? No, this is something new. INVADERS. A lot of them."

"Something new," Walt said.

"I can hear them, every night. Scratching. Lots of them. And I can see their eyes. THOUSANDS OF GLOWING EYES. I hear them clawing at the walls. Trying to get in. I'VE GOT TO STOP THEM!"

"Calm down, okay?" Walt said, shooting a look at Mrs. Biscuit, who had started to wring her hands in agitation. "They're not getting in. Nothing's getting in."

"Do you want to talk about it?" Butterbean said. "Tell me about your mother. Take some deep cleansing breaths. Go to your happy place."

Walt rolled her eyes. "This isn't the time, Bean."

She looked at Biscuit. "Butterbean's going to be a therapy dog."

"Therapist," Butterbean corrected.

"Whatever," Walt said.

Biscuit leaned over and took some deep cleansing breaths. Then he nodded. "Better. That worked."

From the couch, Mrs. Biscuit suddenly gave a brittle laugh. "I don't suppose you rent those pets of yours out, do you? To keep mine quiet?" She gave another shrill laugh.

"Um, ha-ha," Madison said, edging away slightly. "Sorry, that stinks."

"You said it," Mrs. Biscuit said.

Madison cleared her throat. "Well, thanks for letting us come over, but I guess I was wrong about playing. Maybe they just wanted to sniff? We should get going."

"Shoot," Walt said. "Biscuit, where's a toy? We have to make this look good."

Biscuit jumped off the bench and picked up a tube sock half hidden under the couch. "Here, tug on this sock. I love this sock. It's the best toy ever."

"Yes, socks are wonderful," Butterbean agreed, jumping down and gingerly picking up the other end of the sock. "Walt has some compression socks," she whispered through clenched teeth.

"Yes, but those aren't for playing," Walt said. "Too valuable."

"No kidding," Biscuit said, tugging gently at the sock. "What I wouldn't give for one of those."

"Oh, wait, don't go yet. Look at that! I haven't seen him do that in years!" Mrs. Biscuit said, grabbing Madison by the arm again. "You can stay another minute or two, can't you? Maybe he just wanted some company?"

"Yeah, maybe," Madison agreed. Maybe if she ran extra fast. And skipped packing her lunch. Maybe if she teleported. That would do it. She'd be at school in no time if she teleported.

Walt kept one eye on Madison. "Look, we'll see what we can find out, okay? But in the meantime, you have to shut your mouth."

Butterbean nodded, which was difficult to do while she was pulling on the sock. "What time do you see them? The invaders."

Biscuit jerked the sock violently. "Night, mostly. But I keep up the guard during the day anyway, just in case. Never can be too sure."

Walt nodded. "How's this—we'll find out what's out there at the loading dock. And you keep quiet until we do. Deal?" She watched the tug-of-war carefully. Biscuit was definitely winning. But Walt thought Butterbean was holding back.

"Oh, I know what's out there," Biscuit said, jerking the sock a little too hard. (Butterbean made a note to check all her teeth later.) "Monsters, that's what. I saw SLAVERING JAWS. SLAVERING. I wouldn't be surprised if they had venom. DRIPPING FROM THEIR TEETH."

"Right. We'll find out all about the um, venom," Butterbean said, trying not to lose her grip.

"Just keep your trap shut while we do," Walt said.

"Okay, deal." Biscuit sagged. He let go of the sock, sending Butterbean tumbling backward.

"And um, don't worry about guarding. We're part of a Secret Spy Organization. We'll handle the guarding for you," Walt said. They didn't need that dog losing any more sleep. What he didn't know wouldn't hurt him.

Biscuit sagged even more. "Really?"

"Just hang tight until we report back," Walt said.

"Maybe, um, take a nap while you wait," Butterbean said. Naps were always a good way to pass the time.

"You really are a good therapist, Butterbean," Biscuit said softly. "I feel better already." He curled up in his basket and closed his eyes.

Butterbean trotted over to Madison and tugged on her pants leg. "Come on, Madison! Let's go!" They needed to consult with Oscar and the others right away.

"Oh! Look, she wants to go! Wow, great talking to you got to go bye!" Madison babbled as she scooped up Walt and Butterbean.

"Come back anytime," Mrs. Biscuit said, clutching Madison's arm again. "ANYTIME." She hardly took her eyes off of Biscuit as she held the door open for them. "THANK YOU," she mouthed to Madison as they left.

Madison kept the frozen smile on her face until the door shut. Then she took off in a mad dash toward the elevator.

She didn't think even teleporting would help her now.

– 5 –

"WE'RE NOT RETIRED ANYMORE, ARE WE?" Oscar said, his feathers drooping. "Because we're supposed to be retired, remember? We agreed?" He thought sadly of his extensive to-do list. That list had so many good plans. It didn't have investigating intruders on it anywhere.

Butterbean and Walt had told the others what Biscuit had said as soon as Madison dropped them off. And "dropped them off" was the nice way to put it. Madison had practically pitched them into the apartment, grabbed her book bag, and raced off for the bus before their feet even hit the floor. She didn't seem to remember that Butterbean hadn't actually been for a walk. Butterbean didn't mind, though. Walt had given special one-time permission for the use of her litter box. Butterbean appreciated it.

"We're stealthy spies now, Oscar," Walt said dryly. "Get used to it. We're a Secret Spy Organization, and there's nothing we can do about it."

"Yes. Okay," Oscar sighed. "So slavering-jawed invaders are at the loading dock?" He frowned. "That sounds unlikely. Surely Wallace would've heard something from the loading dock rats?"

"Unless . . ." Polo wrung her hands anxiously. "I mean, could something have happened to them? The loading dock rats?"

"Because slavering jaws, that sounds pretty bad," Marco said. He wasn't entirely sure what "slavering" meant, but it sure didn't sound good.

"And venom, don't forget the venom," Polo piped up.

"Right, the venom," Marco agreed.

Oscar gave a tentative shrug. "Well, we don't want to jump to any conclusions. They're probably all just fine."

"Who's probably just fine?" A voice came from the kitchen. A lip-smacky voice that sounded like it was talking with its mouth full. Chad.

Chad was an octopus who lived on the eighth floor. He was an original member of both their heisting gang and investigative team. He visited the apartment a lot, but he sometimes seemed more interested in the contents of Mrs. Food's refrigerator than their company.

"Guess what, Chad!" Polo said, waving at him. "You're a spy now! We're doing secret spy investigating these days. We've retired from regular investigating," she added, nodding significantly at Oscar. That retired part seemed to be important to him.

"Call it whatever you want," Chad said as he sucked down the last of the herring snacks. "My price has gone up. I'm working for shrimp these days."

"Fine," Oscar said. "One question. Have you heard anything about monsters with slavering jaws at the loading dock?"

Chad snorted. "You mean the rats?"

Oscar frowned. "No, I don't think so."

"Then no," Chad said.

"Have you heard ANYTHING about the loading dock?" Marco asked, his eyes narrowed. Past experience had taught him to be skeptical about Chad's answers. Because sometimes he didn't tell you the truth unless you asked the question in exactly the right way.

"I've heard something about monsters with slavering jaws," Chad said, chucking the herring-snack jar into the recycling bin.

"But you said—" Marco started.

"Who'd you hear that from?" Polo asked, folding her arms suspiciously.

"You guys," Chad smirked. "Just now."

"CHAD!" Polo stomped her foot.

Chad gurgled with laughter and then slid down into the sink. "If you need any spy work done, you know my rates."

Oscar shook his head as Chad disappeared. "And the sad thing is we'll need him. Can we even get shrimp?"

"I can add it to Mrs. Food's grocery delivery," Walt said, stretching. "Okay, so who's up for dealing with the monsters? We should go tonight, right?"

"Oh. We?" Oscar said, shifting awkwardly from one foot to the other. "I just assumed the rats were going to do that. Right?"

Marco and Polo exchanged a worried glance. "You want us to . . . with the slavering . . ." Polo said hesitantly.

"By ourselves?" Marco asked.

"That just makes sense, right?" Oscar said. He didn't quite meet their eyes. "Since you have the vents?"

"Sure, but . . ." Polo nudged Marco in the ribs.

"I mean, maybe we should stay here? We don't want to hog all the spy work," Marco said, wringing his hands anxiously.

"Yeah. And we went last night, sooo . . ." Polo said.

"I don't mind if you hog it," Oscar said. "I hate to ruin your fun."

"Yeah, but . . ." Polo tried to think of a counter argument.

"But we did a really lousy job of passing the message, remember?" Marco said quickly.

"We almost ruined everything," Polo agreed. "So maybe you should check it out, Oscar? So we don't mess it up."

"I see your point," Oscar said slowly. "But you know my feet aren't good in the vents. We need a more stealthy presence. Walt, maybe you . . . ?"

Walt sniffed. "Well, I mean, I COULD, but—"

"I'll go!" Butterbean said. "I'll need help getting out of the apartment, but I'll go down there. I can do some monster therapy. It'll be good practice. I've got my test coming up."

Walt shook her head. "Not a good idea. What about Wallace? Maybe he could check it out?"

"Maybe Wallace could check what out?" Wallace asked, strolling into the living room. He was eating a chunk of banana, and he waved it in the air. "Free banana, right there in the dish! My new apartment is awesome."

"We're talking about the loading dock. Have you heard anything about monsters there? Dripping venom and whatnot?" Polo said.

"Glowing eyes and slavering jaws," Marco added.

"Um, nooooo," Wallace said, lowering the banana. He suddenly seemed to have lost his appetite. "Do they have those there?"

"That's what we're trying to find out. Have the loading dock rats said anything?" Polo asked.

"I haven't seen them lately," Wallace said slowly. Then he gasped. "IS THAT WHY? DID MONSTERS GET THE LOADING DOCK RATS?" He leaned against the edge of the sofa heavily. He'd been so involved in fixing up his new apartment that he hadn't even thought to check in with his friends. And now they'd been eaten. It was all his fault.

"We don't know that, Wallace," Oscar said quietly.

"It's just a possibility," Polo said. "They might not have been eaten."

"Yet," Marco added.

"That's why I'm going down there. To check it out," Butterbean added. "As soon as it gets dark."

"No you're not," Walt said quickly. She didn't trust Butterbean down there by herself. She didn't think there really were monsters, exactly, but whatever was down there could be dangerous. There was no telling what Butterbean might do. "You're not going, Bean."

"Except I am," Butterbean insisted.

Walt gritted her teeth. "Then we're all going."

"Um, I don't think . . ." Oscar started.

"WE'RE ALL GOING," Walt said again.

"Yes. We're all going," Oscar said, snapping his beak shut. He'd learned not to argue when Walt got that tone in her voice. Besides, there was safety in numbers. Surely the monsters couldn't eat them all.

"So we're just doing a quick check?" Oscar said after Madison and Mrs. Food had gone to bed. "We'll just pop down to the loading dock, have a quick look around, and then come right back. Just to put Biscuit's mind at ease. Agreed?"

It had already been a tense night in the apartment. Madison, in particular, had been in a bad mood since she came home from school. She was still irritated at

Walt and Butterbean and showed it by glaring point-edly at them whenever they crossed her path.

From what Butterbean understood, she'd gotten a tardy, which was bad, like getting whacked on the nose with a rolled-up newspaper, except without the newspaper part. Or the whacking. To be honest, Butterbean didn't really understand.

Butterbean had tried to make amends, though, by licking any exposed skin that she could find when-ever Madison went past. But it had been hours before Madison started to soften up. The last thing they wanted to do was get into more trouble.

Butterbean wrinkled her nose. "Agreed."

"Unless we need to do some monster fighting," Marco said. "Then it'll take a little longer. Should we bring weapons?" Not that they had any weapons to bring, but it seemed like something they should con-sider.

Oscar shook his head. He wasn't planning on any monster fighting. "We might need to reassess once we see what we're up against. But this is just a reconnais-sance mission." He paused significantly. "Since we're spies."

"Oooohhh, right," Polo said. "Reconnaissance."

"Reconnaissance, so that means we'll just be snoop-ing around?" Marco asked. "No weapons?"

"Right, no weapons," Oscar said. "Well, except for Walt."

"Anything goes wrong and I'll go for eyes," Walt said. Going for the eyes was her go-to attack method.

"Good. Now as soon as Wallace gets here, we can . . ." Oscar trailed off as he stared in the direction of the couch. Four sets of eyes turned to see what he was looking at. And four sets of jaws dropped simultaneously.

Wallace stood next to the sofa. He blushed when he saw them looking and struck a fashion-type pose. "Hi, guys! What do you think?"

"What do I think?" Oscar was dumbfounded. He didn't even have words to describe what he was seeing.

"What are you WEARING? Are those CLOTHES?" Walt said, squinting her eyes, as if that might change things.

"Well, um, yeah," Wallace said, fiddling with his outfit. "Kind of. I mean, do you like it?"

Wallace was wearing a rat-sized sailor shirt complete with dark blue neckerchief around the collar. It was a little bit big for him and hung around his knees, but he made it work. He posed again, ending with a twirl that made the collar swing out in the back.

"What IS that?" Butterbean said, pressing her nose against the fabric and almost knocking Wallace over. "Is that a sailor shirt?"

Wallace blushed again. "Um, yeah, I think that's what you call it. Looks good, right?"

"But where did you get it?" Marco said, rushing over to examine it too. He'd never seen a rat in clothes before, not in real life.

"Do you think it comes in a small?" Polo said, right behind him. She'd never really considered wearing clothes, but now that she saw Wallace in an outfit, her whole outlook had changed.

"Maybe? I don't know." Wallace shrugged. "It was a gift."

"Okay, Wallace, spill it. Where did you get the clothes?" Walt said, lashing her tail impatiently.

Wallace shifted uncomfortably under her stare.

"Mrs. Power Walker. She left it out for me," he said. "She's just nice like that."

"Left it out for you?" Oscar said. "Or just left it out? There's a difference, you know."

Wallace shrugged again. "Well, it wasn't labeled or anything. But she left it on the table, so I just ASSUMED . . ."

"You can't assume!" Oscar squawked, puffing his feathers out.

"Wallace, she'll notice it's gone. You have to put it back," Walt said. "She might enjoy doing cute things for fairies—"

"Brownies," Wallace interrupted.

"Remember? I told you." Butterbean nodded. "Like flat—"

"Flat cake, sure," Walt said, gritting her teeth. "But Wallace, if she figures out she's got a rat in her apartment I can guarantee you she won't be happy. No matter how nice she seems now."

Wallace made a face and stared at the floor. "Well, duh," he said. "I know I can't KEEP it. I just thought I could wear it a little. Just for tonight. You know, as a disguise."

"That's a great idea!" Polo said, her eyes gleaming. "We should all wear disguises! OOOHHH what should I go as?"

"Next time," Oscar said, looking at the clock. It was already getting late. If they were going, they needed to go. They didn't have time to raid Mrs. Food's closet for disguises, especially since there wasn't likely to be much that would fit. "We'll figure out disguises next time." He wondered if there was a way they could go back to regular investigating. The spy stuff seemed to require a lot more accessories. "Come on, Chad's waiting." He didn't even want to think about how much shrimp this was going to cost them.

"Okay, but don't forget. Disguises are important," Polo said, fiddling with the sparkly button she wore around her neck. It suddenly seemed kind of inadequate.

"Sure," Oscar said, hopping over and opening his cage door. "Now, everyone remember how this works?"

They'd snuck out of the apartment a few times before, and they had a system for getting out and back in again. It had worked pretty well so far. (Not that they'd actually tested it that much.) He just hoped it would keep working.

Oscar flew over to the kitchen counter and picked up a dry-cleaning flyer while Walt jumped up on the handle to the front door. Once she'd managed to jiggle it open, Butterbean and the rats squeezed out into the hallway while Oscar followed them, making sure to keep the flyer between the latch and the doorframe as he flew. The door couldn't lock if there was a flyer blocking the latch.

Oscar waited until the door swung closed on the paper, and then he landed on Butterbean's head.

"Okay, rats, hop up," Walt said as Butterbean pushed the elevator button. The rats climbed awkwardly onto her back like she was some kind of feline pony ride. "Let's just hope the elevator is empty," she muttered. "I don't know how we'd explain old Cap'n Wallace over here."

"Hey!" Wallace squealed as he adjusted the hem of his shirt. "It's a good look!"

They only had to wait a few minutes before the elevator bell dinged. They all held their breath and peered inside as the doors opened.

It was empty.

Wallace sagged in relief. He didn't want to admit it, but he hadn't really thought the disguise thing through. Walt was right—a sailor rat would be hard to explain.

"So far so good," Oscar said as they crept into the elevator. "Let's just hope our luck holds."

Butterbean stood up and nosed the button for the basement. They'd never been down there before, so she wasn't entirely sure what to expect. And it was hard to believe that the building had been attacked by evil invaders. But Biscuit was usually a pretty reliable dog. He'd never lied before, not even when Butterbean had asked him if her new collar was too flashy. (It was. Mrs. Food had picked out a hot pink and lime green design. Butterbean was glad when she outgrew it.)

"Basement," the elevator voice said.

"Here goes nothing," Walt said, taking a deep breath as the doors opened.

They stepped out into a wide cinder-block hallway, lit only with dim safety lights spaced along the ceiling every few feet.

"There's a light switch somewhere, but I never use it," Wallace said, looking around awkwardly. He was in between Marco and Polo, and it was hard to see over Marco's big head. "I think it's mostly for humans."

The elevator doors closed behind them. Oscar cleared his throat. He didn't like how quiet it was. "So the loading dock is at the end of this hallway?" He'd be glad when this was over.

"Well, first the storage room, then the loading dock," Wallace said nervously. His voice sounded weird and echoey in the hallway.

Oscar nudged Butterbean with one foot. "Right. Let's go."

Slowly they moved as a group toward a door at the

end of the hall. They had only taken a few steps when a shadow loomed up in front of them.

There was something in their way. Something that hadn't been there a few seconds before. Something that seemed to come out of nowhere.

Chad.

His tentacles were folded, and he was tapping them in irritation as he changed color to become visible. "You're late."

"Don't DO that!" Polo gasped, clutching Walt's fur tightly to keep from falling over backward. She would never get used to Chad showing up like that.

"What the heck, Chad!" Marco squealed. No matter how many times he'd seen it, Chad's cloaking abilities still surprised him every time.

"Give us some warning next time, Chad," Oscar said smoothing his feathers. He had to admit, he'd been a little thrown. (He was lucky that he hadn't fallen off of Butterbean's head entirely.) "Is there a problem? Walt said you knew how to unlock the stor-age room door."

"Oh, I can unlock it. I know the key code," Chad said, wiggling his tentacles. "There's not a place in this building I can't access. But I didn't know how you wanted to handle THEM."

He waved a tentacle at the door in the distance.

And for the first time, Oscar and the others saw the problem.

The problem wasn't the door. It was what was surrounding the door.

In the darkness, the safety lights illuminated what looked like dozens of glowing eyes.

– 6 –

"GLOWING EYES," BUTTERBEAN GASPED. IT was just like Biscuit had described.

"I can't see any slavering jaws," Polo whispered. "Are there slavering jaws?"

"I don't know," Marco whispered back. "I don't even know what slavering is."

"It's a scary kind of slobbering," Walt said. "Hold tight." She waited as the rats flattened themselves against her, holding on to her fur. Then she arched her back and got into a crouch position. She wasn't sure how she was going to go for the eyes with three rats on her back, but she was willing to give it a shot. There was no shortage of targets, that was for sure.

"Wait, let me see if I can get a better look," Oscar said. He peered down the hallway at the eyes. There were a lot of them, but whatever they were, they were smaller than he'd anticipated. From what Biscuit had said, he was expecting something big. Bigger than Biscuit, anyway. (Not that that was very big. Biscuit was kind of tiny, to be honest.)

"I'm going in," he said, launching himself off of Butterbean's head. He flew closer to the door, keeping out of range of the eyes. He frowned. The closer he got, the more it seemed like he was looking at—

"Wallace? Is that you?" A thin voice echoed down the hallway. One of the pairs of glowing eyes separated from the group and moved closer to Butterbean and the other pets.

Wallace sat up straight on Walt's back. "It's me. Who's there?"

A small shape came out of the shadows. Oscar frowned from overhead. Yes, it certainly seemed like he was looking at—

"DUNKIN?" Wallace gasped, letting go of Walt's fur and sliding off her back. "Is that you? What are you DOING here? You're INSIDE!"

Oscar nodded to himself. Yep, they were definitely rats.

Wallace rushed over to Dunkin the rat and squeezed

him in a tight hug. Then he grabbed him by the arm and dragged him back toward Butterbean and Walt. "Guys! Guys! This is Dunkin, my friend from the loading dock. He's one of the loading dock rats!" He hugged Dunkin again. "We thought you'd been eaten!" Wallace waved his arms at Oscar overhead. "You can land, Oscar. It's my loading dock rat friends!"

Oscar turned back and landed carefully on Butterbean's head. Even in the dark, the concrete floors of the basement looked a little too slippery for his taste. The last thing he wanted to do was embarrass himself by making a crash landing.

"But what are you doing inside?" Wallace said, frowning. "You're a loading dock rat. Why aren't you on the loading dock?"

"Is that a nightgown?" Dunkin said, touching the sleeve of Wallace's sailor shirt.

"What? No! This is a disguise." Wallace smoothed the front of his shirt.

"We're spies!" Polo said, sliding down from Walt's back and hurrying over to where Wallace was standing. "We were going to all have disguises, but Oscar says that'll have to wait until next time." When she got about a foot away, she suddenly stopped short. Even if he was Wallace's friend, Dunkin was still a wild rat. And she never knew what to expect from wild rats. "Why aren't you on the loading dock?"

"Funny story there," Dunkin said, shifting nervously from one foot to the other. He didn't say it like it was really funny, though. If Polo didn't know any better, she would've thought he sounded scared. But loading dock rats didn't get scared. Did they?

"So, you know I love the loading dock. Lived there my whole life. I'm in charge of all the community activities. You know my story, Wallace," he said.

"Dunkin was born in a doughnut box," Wallace said knowingly.

"Right," Dunkin said. "So you know I wouldn't just LEAVE. But lately, the loading dock has become a little . . . well, let's say unsafe."

"Okay, that's understandable, I guess," Wallace

said. If the loading dock wasn't safe, of course the rats would leave. "But why didn't you just hide out in the storage room?" Wallace said. That's what they used to do sometimes, when the weather was particularly bad. Make a party of it. The Strathmore Building had some pretty sloppy insulation around its exhaust venting.

"Well, we were. But that stopped feeling safe too," Dunkin said, shifting his weight.

"It's the slavering jaws, isn't it," Marco said knowingly.

"Um. You could say that," Dunkin said. "We don't feel welcome there anymore. None of us do."

"Wait. There really are SLAVERING JAWS?" Butterbean's nose trembled.

"Maybe? There are definitely jaws. Take a look for yourself." He waved at the door.

Oscar cocked his head. "Oh, I don't know if we—"

"Guys, let them through. They want to see for themselves," Dunkin called to the glowing eyes around the door. "Oh, sorry, let me introduce you. Guys, you know Wallace. And these are his friends, um, Dog, Cat, Bird, and Other Rats. Wallace, this is the gang from the loading dock. Lego, Waffle, Folger, Snapple, Pocky, Dave, Cheerio, Mike, and Ike. And oh yeah, Ken. Wave hello, Ken!"

A rat under the exit sign waved a tentative hello.

"So, yeah, just go take a look," Dunkin said. "It's not a great situation. Any advice would be appreciated."

Oscar glanced over at Walt, who shrugged. "Lead the way, Dunkin."

Dunkin gave a small shrill laugh. "Oh no, I'm not going with you. We'll all stay here. But you feel free. Knock yourself out."

Oscar gritted his beak. Whatever was out there couldn't be that bad. "Fine. Chad?"

Chad uncloaked and slithered his way over to the keypad. "Space, please, I need my space," he snarled at the rats, who scattered as he got closer.

Chad hoisted himself up and typed on the keypad. The door buzzed quietly.

"Oh, going in the human way, huh? Well, that's new," Dunkin said, watching from a safe distance.

Chad hung on to the exit sign with one tentacle as he tugged the door open with another one. "Any cameras inside?"

"Um, yes, there's a surveillance camera aimed at the door. I think it's mostly for humans. I don't think it's aimed right to see you all."

"Got it," Chad said, dangling from the sign. He snapped one of his free tentacles at Butterbean. "I'm not holding this for my health, okay?"

"Oh! Sorry!" Butterbean raced forward and squeezed

into the gap in the door. Oscar barely had time to tighten his grip before they were skidding to a stop in the storage room.

"Make it snappy," Chad called after them. "I'll be right here."

Walt squeezed in behind Butterbean (with Marco and Polo back on board) and stood silently in the large storage room. Tall cagelike storage units lined the walls and went almost all the way from floor to ceiling. They were filled with shadowy boxes, bags, and random pieces of furniture.

"One of these belongs to Mrs. Food," Butterbean said, her nose quivering in the air. "I'm not sure which one, though. I think she keeps her holiday decorations here. Want me to find it?"

"It's not important," Oscar said quietly. "I don't think the storage units are the problem."

The room had seemed silent when they first came in, but the longer they stood there, the more they noticed a small background sound. A scrabbling sound. It was coming from the large metal door at the end of the storage area. The sound of something trying to get in.

"That's the door to the loading dock?" Oscar asked, examining it cautiously.

"That's it," Wallace said. He wished he hadn't worn the sailor shirt. It's not like it was really a disguise anyway. He would've been much better off as an anonymous naked rat.

"I can see why the rats didn't feel safe," Polo said in a small voice.

"That door looks pretty solid," Oscar said, cocking his head. "Even if something wanted to get in, I don't think it could get through that."

"Something definitely wants to get in," Walt said under her breath.

"Let's go." Oscar nodded toward the door. Taking a deep breath, they crept slowly toward the door at the end of the room. The scrabbling sound got louder. When they were standing directly opposite the door, Walt had finally had enough.

"Okay, where's it coming from?" Walt's ears swiveled around as she scanned the room. "It can't get in though the metal door. So where is it?"

"There," Wallace said, swallowing hard. He pointed up at an exhaust pipe that disappeared into a hole in the wall near the door. The insulation around the pipe looked like it was moving.

"That's not rats, is it, Wallace?" Butterbean whispered.

"I don't think so," Wallace said, his eyes on the pipe. "Rats would've said something by now."

As they watched, a puff of insulation fell out onto the floor. Then a second puff.

And then, slowly, a small long-fingered hand reached out into the room and felt around on the wall surrounding the hole.

"That's a HAND!" Butterbean gasped.

"No kidding," Walt said. But her whiskers trembled when she said it.

Oscar felt a chill. "I know what that is. Go back!"

Butterbean took a step closer and peered up at the tiny hand, which was actively digging away at the insulation.

"Go," Oscar snapped. "I've seen hands like that on the Television. I know what we're dealing with now."

Walt looked up at him. "What?"

Oscar's face looked grim. "Raccoons. The Strathmore's being invaded by raccoons."

— 7 —

"RACCOONS? LET ME TALK TO THEM," Butterbean said. "I can handle this." She'd never met any raccoons before, but she liked their stripey tails, and she could start out by mentioning that. Everybody liked compliments.

Walt shot Oscar a panicked look. She didn't know a lot about raccoons, but she did know Butterbean. She didn't like the odds.

Besides, if Oscar was freaked out, Walt was freaked out. "No, Bean, not here. Let's go back and discuss."

"But—" Butterbean protested.

"Discuss! Now!" Oscar said, flying over to the door,

where Chad was still hanging limply, drumming his free tentacles against the doorframe.

"FINE," Butterbean grumbled, turning around and stomping after him.

"Oh, you're back," Chad said in a bored tone. "Any time you're ready. Take all the time you need. Don't mind me."

"I think that's sarcasm," Polo whispered to Marco as she held tight to Walt's fur.

"I think you're right," Marco whispered back as they went through the doorway.

Butterbean squeezed through after Walt, just barely making it before Chad slammed the door. "Ooh, so sorry. That must've slipped." He smirked as he dangled from the exit sign.

Oscar didn't pay any attention to Chad. He brushed past, landing on the floor in front of Butterbean and Walt. (Badly. He was right about the floor. It was way more slippery than he was comfortable with.) Dunkin and the other rats weren't anywhere to be found. (Oscar couldn't help but be relieved about that. He was glad his landing hadn't had an audience.)

Oscar cleared his throat. "Look, Butterbean, I know you want to help, but the situation has changed. I've seen programs about raccoons. I know what they're like. They're not to be trusted. They're thieves. They destroy property." He looked at the others significantly. "They have . . ." He paused. "A REPUTATION."

Butterbean put on her best shocked face. (The situation seemed to call for it.)

Marco and Polo exchanged a look.

Oscar frowned at them. "What?" he said in irritation. "You don't trust my sources? Believe me, I've done my research. I don't say these things lightly."

Polo squirmed. "It's not that," she said, not meeting Oscar's eyes. "It's just . . . well . . ." She trailed off and looked over to Marco.

"See, rats also have a reputation," Marco said slowly.

"It's a bad reputation," Polo said. She wrung her hands together. "I don't know if it's raccoon bad. But it's bad."

"Some people don't like rats," Marco whispered.

"Hmm." Oscar frowned. They had a point. He had seen several programs about rats that were less than complimentary, it was true.

"Have you ever met a raccoon?" Walt asked after a minute.

"Well, no," Oscar said. "Not personally."

He looked over at Marco and Polo and Wallace in his tiny sailor top. The rats on the Television never wore tiny sailor tops. Maybe Marco and Polo were right. Maybe he was being unfair and judgmental. He hadn't really given the raccoons a chance. But then he remembered that hand poking out through the insulation. He shivered.

"Just let me talk to them," Butterbean said, looking up at Oscar hopefully. "I'm sure I can therapy the situation."

"That's not how therapy dogs work, Bean," Walt groaned. She didn't know how many times she was going to have to explain this.

"No, Bean, it's too risky," Oscar said, staring up at the door. If he were smart, he would go right back upstairs and let Butterbean explain the situation to Biscuit in the morning. If he were smart, he'd leave the loading dock rats to fend for themselves. But he had a feeling he wasn't going to be smart. And he had a worse feeling that Butterbean was never going to give up.

"We shouldn't mess with raccoons, Oscar," Walt said in a low voice. "This isn't some imaginary ghost situation. This could be dangerous." They'd dealt with sketchy situations in the past, but never situations that put them in real physical danger. (Well, except for once or twice.)

Oscar looked at Walt and nodded. They should definitely go home. Leave it alone. Messing with raccoons was always a bad idea.

"Walt is right, Bean," Oscar said. "It could be

dangerous." He took a deep breath. "So I should be the one to talk to the raccoons. I'm the only one who can make a quick escape if I need to." He made elaborate flapping motions. "Wings. See?"

Butterbean nodded. "Right. Wings." Oscar had a point. She didn't have wings. Any escape she made would have to be on foot. It wouldn't necessarily be quick.

"Oscar, seriously?" Walt said, stepping in front of the door. "We can't go in there! They'll be through that hole in no time. Didn't you see that hand?"

Oscar flexed his wings. "It'll be fast. I'll reason with them. Surely they'll understand. And then we can at least say we tried. Chad? Can you get the doors?"

Chad rolled his eyes. "We're talking extra shrimp. Jumbo." He tapped the code in again and then opened the door. Then he hesitated. "Wait, doors? What do you mean doors?"

"I mean both doors," Oscar said. "I'm not stopping at the storage room. I'm going out onto the loading dock."

"Tell me again why you're doing this?" Walt said to Oscar as they stood in front of the loading dock door. "Because this is a BAD idea. Capital B-A-D."

"I know," Oscar said in low voice. "But you know Butterbean isn't going to let this go. If we leave now, we'll just have to come back later. And who knows what the raccoons will be doing then."

"Fine. But I don't like it," Walt muttered. Oscar was right—Butterbean could be very stubborn. And those raccoons had already made it pretty far.

"Besides, if my motivational speech works, we've saved the day. If not, we're not any worse off, and we leave it for someone else to solve." Oscar was secretly very proud of his motivational speaking skills. It was a natural talent he had.

"I guess so," Walt said. She still had a bad feeling about the whole thing. Mostly because she didn't think Oscar was as good at motivational speeches as he thought he was. And she kept remembering that little wiry hand poking through the insulation. She just hoped she was wrong.

"You're *sure* you don't want me to do it?" Butterbean said, trotting up behind them. "I can totally go. I have a winning personality." She'd heard that in the elevator more than once, mostly when she was about to get a treat.

"No, I'll handle it," Oscar said. "Chad, remember to be ready with the door."

Chad dangled overhead and gave what was probably

supposed to be an agreeable nod. It was hard to tell with him upside down.

"Remember," Oscar said. "Open the door, let me out, and close it. And don't open it again until I tap three times." He didn't like having the door closed behind him, but it was the only way they could be sure the raccoons wouldn't rush the building.

"Right, sure, tap tap, et cetera," Chad said, inspecting one of his tentacles.

"Good." Oscar hoped Chad was paying attention. You could never be sure with him.

"Ready, Oscar?" Marco rubbed Oscar's shoulders like he'd seen a boxing manager do on TV once. He wasn't entirely sure where Oscar's shoulders were, so he rubbed around the whole lower neck area and then patted Oscar awkwardly on the back. Oscar seemed to appreciate it.

"Ooh! Take this for luck!" Polo said, slipping something over Oscar's head.

Oscar hardly noticed. He was focused on taking deep cleansing breaths. He couldn't mess this up. Finally he stood up straight and tall.

"Okay, Chad," Oscar said. "NOW!"

Chad entered the key code with one tentacle while he pulled on the door handle with another. The door opened just enough for Oscar to squeeze through.

Taking one last deep breath, Oscar stepped outside. Chad let the door swing shut behind him.

"What did you give him?" Marco asked Polo as they watched Oscar go.

"My button," Polo said. "It'll bring him good luck."

"Wait." Walt turned slowly to Polo, the fur on her neck rising. "Your SPARKLY button?"

"Uh-huh," Polo said proudly. "It'll help."

"Oh no." Walt looked at the door in horror. But it was too late. The door had shut. Oscar was gone. "Oh no."

Oscar heard the door click shut behind him. He was on his own.

The scrabbling sounds had stopped as soon as Chad had opened the door, but Oscar knew the raccoons weren't gone. They were there. Watching him. Waiting.

He cleared his throat and spoke to the empty loading dock. "Ahem. Loading dock raccoons! My name is Oscar, and you may consider me to be a representative of the Strathmore Building. As representative, and as a resident, I request that you vacate the premises immediately."

He tried to sound as official as possible, but he wasn't sure he was pulling it off.

He waited for some reaction, but there was none, just silence.

Oscar cleared his throat a second time and took a tentative step forward, careful to avoid the gaps in the metal slats below his feet. He'd only been there a few minutes, but he could already tell that he was not a fan of this loading dock.

"Attention, raccoons!" He tried again. "Raccoon friends!" He thought the "friends" part was a nice touch. "This is your Strathmore Building representative, Oscar, asking you to please find a new gathering place. You are disturbing the residents inside. This is your last warning. Please leave."

"SHINY." A soft voice wafted through the air. Oscar looked sharply to the side, but he couldn't see anyone there.

"Please don't make me tell you again," Oscar said, his voice shaking slightly. "You need to leave immediately."

He took another step forward. Whatever Polo had given him bumped softly against his chest, and he looked down quickly. His eyes widened.

There was one thing all of the raccoon programs on the Television had made perfectly clear. Raccoons couldn't resist sparkly things. And there was nothing more sparkly than Polo's button.

"Um, please leave by morning. That is our request." Oscar tried to cover the button with his feathers, but it was too big to hide. "Thank you for your attention. Best wishes, good luck for the future, that will be all," Oscar said, scrambling backward toward the door. But before he could reach it, a small thin hand reached out from between the loading dock slats and grabbed his foot.

"URK!" Oscar gurgled, looking down. The hand that gripped his foot was just like the one that had reached out through the insulation in the storage room. And it wasn't the only one. Dozens of tiny hands were reaching up in between the slats, feeling around the loading dock, and grabbing at whatever they could find. And the only thing to find was Oscar.

"SO SPARKLY." Another voice drifted up from underneath the loading dock.

"OOOOOhhhhhhhh." There was a chorus of giggles. "Mine, please."

"Yes, very sparkly, ha-ha, thank you!" Oscar shook his foot desperately, but as soon as he'd freed one foot, a hand latched onto the other. Panicked, Oscar launched himself into the air, pulling against the raccoon holding him down.

In one huge effort, he jerked his leg free and shot up into the sky. He looked down just in time to see raccoons swarming onto the loading dock from all sides, looking up at him with glowing eyes and outstretched hands.

Oscar swerved around and flew directly into the loading dock door, tapping against it repeatedly.

The door opened a crack. One eye peered out. "Was that three taps? We agreed to three taps." Chad's voice came through the crack.

"Yes, that was three! You know it's me. LET ME IN!" Oscar yelled, beating his wings against the door. He glanced back just as one large raccoon rose up out of the group on the loading dock.

"You don't make the rules around here, OSCAR," the raccoon said in a deep, echoing voice. "I don't like being told what to do. Better fly away while you still can." He laughed a low, booming laugh, which was immediately accompanied by giggles from the other raccoons half-hidden in the shadows.

Oscar cringed. That was the authoritative voice he'd been trying for earlier. No wonder the raccoons hadn't listened to him.

He crashed against the door again, just as Chad's eye disappeared, and the door swung open another inch. Oscar threw himself at the gap, managing to squeeze inside (only losing a feather or two in the process).

He could still hear the big raccoon laughing as the door swung shut behind him.

"So what did they say?" Butterbean asked, sniffing at Oscar's foot as he collapsed in a heap in front of them. She blinked at him expectantly.

"I'm guessing it didn't go well," Walt said, wrapping her tail around her feet.

"You could say that," Oscar said.

"We heard laughing," Polo said. "Did they agree to go away?"

"Not exactly," Oscar said, scrambling to his feet. "I don't think they're leaving."

He ducked his head so that Polo's button slipped off his neck and onto the floor. "They did like your button, though." He didn't have the heart to tell her just how much they'd liked it.

"Well, duh," Polo said, picking it up and putting it back on. "It's beautiful."

Walt raised an eyebrow at Oscar, but he shrugged it off.

"So what do we do now?" Butterbean asked.

"Nothing," Oscar said. "We do nothing. We go home."

"I told the rats we were getting the loading dock back for them," Butterbean said. "They're kind of our clients now. So we need to do SOMETHING."

"We'll see," Oscar said, climbing tiredly onto Butterbean's head. He wasn't worried about disappointing the loading dock rats. He wasn't worried about Biscuit getting evicted. What he was worried about was that raccoon. Because now it knew his name.

– *8* –

THE WHITE CAT WAS LYING ON THE COUCH when they got back.

"Well, that took forever," she said, stretching full length on the cushions.

"You're not supposed to be here! You don't live here!" Polo said in frustration. "Mrs. Food could come out at any minute." They'd managed to navigate the hallways and elevators all the way back without anyone seeing them. The last thing they needed was to get caught because the white cat didn't know how to be careful.

"Relax, it's the middle of the night." The white cat yawned. "No one is coming out."

"It doesn't matter," Marco said, crossing his arms. "It's risky."

"Yeah, yeah. What about him?" The white cat waved a paw at Chad, who had climbed up onto the kitchen counter and was browsing the contents of the refrigerator. (He said all that dangling had made him weak with hunger.) "Or him!" The white cat waved a paw in Wallace's direction. "He's not supposed to be here either, and I'd be a lot easier to explain than a rat in a nightgown."

"It's a sailor shirt, and I'm taking it off," Wallace said. Marco and Polo looked at him with horrified expressions. "As soon as I get home, I mean. Sheesh."

"Well? I want details. What happened in the base-ment?" The white cat sat up expectantly and plumped the couch pillows. "Last I heard there were slavering jaws?"

Wallace nodded. "YES! SLAVERING. It was TERRIBLE."

The white cat cocked her head. "Really!"

Oscar flew up into his cage and landed heavily on his perch. It had been a long night. "So to speak."

"We've got a raccoon situation," Walt said, sitting down in front of the couch. "That's what's upsetting Biscuit."

"And the rats," Wallace added.

"Ooooh, raccoons. That's bad. They'll take over in a heartbeat, right?" The white cat's eyes widened. "I'm guessing you weren't able to talk sense into them."

"Not exactly," Oscar admitted.

"But what about you, Butterbean? Aren't you a therapist now? Surely they listened to you, right?" The white cat seemed to be enjoying herself a little too much.

Butterbean flopped down with a huff. "They WOULD'VE, I'm sure of it. But no one would even let me talk to them!"

"Why not? It's just a couple of raccoons, right?" The white cat shot Walt a look.

"I know, right?" Butterbean whined.

"Cut it out, cat," Walt said.

"But that's just it! It's not just a couple of raccoons—

it's a gang!" Wallace protested. "Slavering jaws, remember? It was a bunch of them. A whole troupe!"

The white cat sat up, looking at Wallace with real curiosity on her face. "Wait, are they a gang or a troupe? Because that's not the same thing."

"Um." Wallace looked at Marco and Polo, who shrugged. "I don't know. Troupe?"

"So they're raccoon performers? A troupe implies singing and dancing." The white cat smoothed her whiskers. "I may need to investigate this. Performing raccoons are an entirely different matter."

"I didn't hear them singing," Wallace said, wringing the hem of his shirt. "But maybe?"

"They're probably a gang," Marco said.

"They were laughing a lot," Polo said thoughtfully.

"Don't remind me," Oscar said grouchily. "Now if you don't mind, cat, it's been a long night, and I—"

But he never finished the sentence. Because at that moment they realized they weren't alone.

Madison was standing in the hallway staring at them with her mouth hanging open. Her hair was sticking up on one side, and she didn't look entirely awake.

"What is the—huh?" She blinked and stared at the white cat. "What."

"Oh shoot," the white cat muttered under her breath.

"I TOLD YOU!" Marco said, throwing his arms

into the air. "Didn't we SAY? I KNEW YOU'D GET CAUGHT."

"Shh, Marco. Be cool. No sudden moves," Polo said, watching Madison blink again. Madison hadn't really reacted—she was still just staring at the white cat, swaying slightly in place. A little drool had formed at the corner of her mouth.

The animals stared back at Madison. No one moved a muscle.

"Huh. That looks like . . . huh," Madison said, yawning and then taking a few steps toward the kitchen, where she stopped short again.

"Oh no," Oscar said under his breath. He shook his head. No matter how sleepy Madison was, there was no way she was going to be able to miss the octopus dangling between the countertop and the refrigerator. Octopuses in the kitchen were always attention grabbers.

She didn't.

"Octopus," Madison said.

Chad didn't even bother freezing in place. He burped, gave her a jaunty salute with one of his free tentacles, and went back to his snacks.

Madison gave a clumsy return salute. "Right. Right," she muttered as she turned around and headed back toward her room. "Octopus. Sure."

She padded down the hallway and disappeared back into her room. The animals sat in silence, afraid to move until they were sure she was gone.

"So, do you think she spotted me?" Chad finally said as Madison's door clicked shut. He chucked the herring jar into the trash.

"Gosh, Chad, I don't know." Walt rolled her eyes. "What do you think?"

"I'll tell you what I think," the white cat said, jumping off the couch. "I think that was a close call. You guys almost got us caught."

"YOU GUYS?" Marco said, outraged. "YOU'RE BLAMING US?"

Walt opened her mouth to protest but decided against it. Some things just weren't worth it.

"Come on, Chad. Clock's a-ticking," the white cat said. "I want to see these so-called performers."

Chad shrugged an elaborate dangling shrug and then dropped down to the floor. "Payment up front."

Oscar frowned. "I really don't think I'd say they were performers. I think Wallace misspoke."

"Well, we'll see. Here." The white cat rooted around behind the couch for a minute and then dragged out a package of cat treats. "How's this for payment? They're brand-new—not even on the market yet. Caviar flavored, super fancy." She tossed the packet in Chad's direction. (It didn't even make it halfway to him. The white cat was never known for her sports prowess.) Chad shot her a cold look before slithering toward it and inspecting the package.

The white cat smirked at Walt. "It's part of my gig with Beautiful Buffet Cat Food. I'm starring in the classic commercials, of course, but they also want me promoting this new line. It's a pretty big deal."

"Really," Walt said.

"It's caviar flavored. Super fancy," the white cat said again.

"So you said." Walt said.

"UREREERRRKKKKK." A loud hacking noise came from the other side of the room.

Chad had turned an interesting shade of green.

A cat treat shot out of his mouth and landed wetly on the floor in front of them. He gagged a few more times and then threw the treat package against the wall. "Not on your life."

The white cat sagged. "Yeah, they're pretty terrible. Well, it was worth a try." She leaned conspiratorially toward Walt. "Honestly, I don't know how I'm going to choke them down. But I guess that's why they pay me the big bucks. Acting."

Walt stalked over to the cat treat package and sniffed it. Then she curled her lip and kicked it under the couch. "Good luck with that."

The white cat shrugged and sashayed toward the vent. "Watch and learn. I know how to talk to performers. I'll get this raccoon situation fixed and be back before you know it."

She disappeared into the vents, with Chad slithering along behind her.

"That's what I'm afraid of," Oscar said under his breath.

The white cat burst out of the vent in the Strathmore basement and immediately struck a dramatic pose. That was for the benefit of the rats, who she had been informed would be milling around the area, in desperate need of entertainment. The white cat was never one to disappoint a waiting audience. But her information was apparently wrong. There were no rats to be seen.

"Humph," the white cat grumbled, smoothing her whiskers and looking around casually in case she'd overlooked someone. But no. The basement was empty. She was glad she hadn't gone with her original entrance idea. (High stepping and jazz hands.)

Faint noises were coming from the other side of the large metal door. The white cat nodded at it. "Storage room, I presume?"

Chad nodded. "Yup."

The white cat fluffed up her fur and did some warm-up stretches. Then she turned to Chad.

"Listen, legs. When I give you the cue, open the door as wide as possible. I want to make a spectacular entrance. Really dazzle them." Once those raccoons got a glimpse of a real celebrity, they'd be putty in her hands. And if they really were a troupe, it was always good to have backup dancers on call. As long as they knew she was the star. "Got it?"

"Sure, sure," Chad grumbled. "Entrance blah blah. Dazzle dazzle." He climbed up onto the exit sign and dangled one tentacle in front of the keypad. "But you owe me decent food. None of those treats of yours."

The white cat snorted. "Trust me, I've got a whole seafood platter with your name on it." She smoothed the fur on her forehead in the shape of a curl and stepped onto the small mat in front of the storage room. Then she put on her best stage face. Her eyes were practically twinkling in the dim light. "And . . . action!"

Chad started to enter the code into the keypad. But before he could finish, the door abruptly opened, leaving him awkwardly hanging in the doorway.

A small raccoon wearing a sequined tube top stood just inside the door and stared at them, unblinking. Behind her, the room was filled with raccoons. More raccoons than the white cat had ever imagined. Raccoons were clinging to the wire walls of the storage units. They had broken into one and were rummaging around in a suitcase filled with clothes. Three were wearing hats (two baseball, one cowboy), one was playing a ukulele (badly, you could tell he hadn't had lessons), and one had a thick cashmere scarf wrapped multiple times around his neck (you could hardly see his face, it was wrapped so high).

"Who's that? What do they want?" A high squeaky voice came from the middle of the suitcase-raccoon pack. (The white cat thought it was the raccoon in the cowboy hat, but she wasn't sure.)

"What do you want?" the tube-top raccoon asked.

"Um. I . . ." The white cat swallowed hard. She didn't usually get stage fright, especially when it was a performance as important as this one. But she hadn't

been prepared for this. Even Chad was speechless. He was still dangling motionless overhead, his eyes wide.

"I'm a celebrity," she finally said.

"She's a celebrity," Chad echoed.

"Oh. Congrats," the raccoon said. There was an awkward silence as they stared at each other.

A raccoon wearing a snorkel mask pushed up on his forehead appeared in the doorway. Without a word, he reached down and grabbed the small mat under the white cat's feet and tugged it out from under her. Then, hugging it close to his chest, he ran away into the shadows on his hind legs.

"Nope," the white cat said, turning around. "Nopey nope nope." This was not what she'd signed up for. This was not an appreciative audience.

The white cat made sure she kept her steps even and calm until she heard the door shut behind her. Then she shot into the vent at top speed, running so fast that her feet hardly touched the floor. Once she was safely inside, she whirled around, the fur on her back bristling. Chad squelched into the vent after her. (He was not nearly as fast.)

"Give me a rave review, and I'll double your salary," she said as Chad pulled himself inside. "I was fabulous. Dazzling performance. You were blown away. Deal?"

Chad took a moment to consider. He could always use some extra shrimp. "Deal."

"So?" Oscar opened one eye when he heard the white cat creep back in.

"Amateurs," the white cat said, blowing air out of her nose. "Nothing but a bunch of amateurs. Hardly worth the trip."

"So are they gone?" Walt asked.

"Are they a troupe?" Polo asked, poking her nose out of her cedar chip pile.

"Do they need therapy?" Butterbean asked hopefully. "I'm still available."

"No, who knows, and probably," the white cat said. "And now I'm leaving. They're hardly worth my time. Although . . . Chad?" She looked expectantly at Chad, who was halfway to the kitchen sink. "Don't you have something to add?"

Chad looked around and then nodded. "Right. She was fabulous. Amazing. Eight tentacles up," he said in a deadpan voice as climbed into the sink and slid down the drain.

"See? Well, I'm leaving. I've got a photo shoot tomorrow," the white cat said, turning to leave. Then she hesitated. "Oh. You might be interested in knowing.

Those raccoons have taken over the storage area. They're going through everyone's stuff. Anyway, cheers!" She disappeared.

Walt looked up at Oscar. "Well, that's not good."

Oscar sighed. "It's not our problem. I'm sorry, but we need to stay out of it."

"But . . ." Butterbean started, but Oscar held up one wing.

"Butterbean. This is a large number of raccoons, whatever we call them. We're just a group of seven pets."

Butterbean sat up. "Excuse me, but we're an International Crime Syndicate and Investigator Gang," she said indignantly.

"And spies," Marco said sleepily from the top of the water bottle. "Don't forget spies."

"Well. True. But as spies, we need to know when to fade into the background. This is one of those times. Let someone else clean up the mess for once." Oscar puffed his feathers out. "Besides, I'm sure this will all blow over soon. Trust me. You'll see."

He tucked his head under his wing.

He didn't realize how wrong he was.

– 9 –

"Wow, I had the WEIRDEST dream last night," Madison said to Mrs. Food at breakfast the next morning. Five sets of eyes slowly turned to look at her. "I was in the living room, right? And there was a ghost cat and a tiny little sailor, who I think was a mouse or something? Maybe a squirrel? And all the pets were there, and they were just staring at me. Kind of like . . ." Madison trailed off as she looked into the living room. ". . . that."

Butterbean was listening so intently that she had forgotten to chew and had kibble dribbling out of her mouth. Walt had paused midlick with one paw extended. Marco and Polo had their faces pressed up to the side of their cage (with unintentionally hilarious results). Oscar was frozen with one foot hovering over his food dish.

When they noticed Madison noticing them, they immediately unfroze and pretended to be engrossed in their activities. (Marco and Polo didn't really have any activity to pretend to do, so they just inspected the side of their cage thoughtfully.)

"Huh." Madison frowned. Then she turned back to Mrs. Food. "But then I was in the kitchen and—"

There was a knock at the front door.

"Did they say anything? The animals?" Mrs. Food took a piece of toast as Madison jumped up from the table.

"I don't think so. But it was so real! And oh! There was an octopus!" Madison opened the front door. Bob the maintenance man was standing in the doorway holding a clipboard.

"Oh, hi," Madison said. "Mrs. Fudeker? It's Bob." Madison smiled quickly at Bob and then stepped back so he could come inside.

Butterbean stopped eating again, dribbling more kibble. Too many interesting things were happening. There was no way she could concentrate on food.

Bob pretty much ran things at the Strathmore Building. He had a history with Butterbean and Walt. He'd always been more than a little suspicious of their activities, but he'd never found any concrete evidence to hold against them. (Butterbean had concrete reasons for being suspicious of Bob, but she kept them to herself.)

"Sorry to bother you all so early," Bob said, clearing his throat. "So. It looks like we've had an incident down in the storage room. A lady on the sixth floor has made a complaint."

"Probably Mrs. Hates Dogs on Six," Butterbean whispered darkly. "She complains about EVERY-THING."

Bob consulted his clipboard. "She says the valuables in her storage unit have been ransacked, and some things are missing. We're planning to set up additional cameras, but in the meantime, you might want to check and see if you're missing any items."

"Wow, that's terrible!" Madison said.

"Yes, terrible." Mrs. Food looked concerned. "We'll go down today and take a look. Make sure everything's there."

"Good, good." Bob made a check mark on his clipboard. "Hopefully it's just some kind of mistake."

"A mistaken ransacking?" Madison wrinkled her nose. "Does that ever happen?"

Bob shrugged. "No, but who knows. Just between us, this lady? She complains a lot."

"I knew it!" Butterbean barked. "Mrs. Hates Dogs on Six! It has to be!"

"Butterbean! Shh!" Mrs. Food frowned at Butterbean. "Thanks for telling us. We'll let you know if we spot any problems."

"Gotcha. Thanks. I'll let myself out." Bob turned and left, shooting Butterbean a sharp look as he closed the door. Butterbean ignored it.

"Madison, would you mind going down after school and taking a look? Just see if anything looks out of place," Mrs. Food said, sitting back down and examining her cold toast before finally rejecting it.

"Sure," Madison said, grabbing her book bag. "But like Bob said, hopefully it's nothing. See you later!" She swung the backpack over her shoulders and hurried out.

"Well, it's not nothing," Oscar said, watching as Mrs. Food put the breakfast dishes in the dishwasher and headed down the hallway to her office. "It's those raccoons."

"You can say that again, buster," Dunkin the loading dock rat said as he sauntered into the living room.

"DUNKIN?" Kibble bounced onto the floor at Butterbean's feet. It was not turning out to be a successful breakfast time.

"What are you doing here? You can't be here!" Polo

climbed up onto the water bottle to survey the room. "This is Mrs. Food's apartment!"

Dunkin put his hands on his hips as he looked around the room. "We're your clients, right? Well, we need a place to stay, and I have to say, this looks pretty good." Dunkin clapped his hands loudly. "It's okay, make yourselves at home, guys."

A small group of rats peeked out from behind the couch. They watched for a few seconds, assessing the situation, and then scattered, scurrying to various locations around the room.

"WHAT? What's HAPPENING?" Polo squealed as a rat shimmied up the side of her cage and hopped into a pile of cedar chips next to her.

"Mind if I help myself?" A small brown rat sidled up to Butterbean and scooped up three stray kibbles. "Can't resist these. They're crazy good."

Butterbean looked at the rat in amazement. "But who are you? Are you a rat from last night? Pizza? Snapple? Mike or Ike?"

The rat snorted. "Pizza? What kind of name is that? No, I'm Lego. But you can call me roomie." He nudged Butterbean in the leg with his elbow.

"ROOMIE?" Butterbean gasped and whipped her head around to look at Oscar. But Oscar looked as horrified as Butterbean felt.

Walt stood up. "Sorry to disappoint you, rats, but no. This is not happening. We're not going to be roomies. You're going to have to stay somewhere else."

"Au contraire, mon frère, we're staying right here." Dunkin folded his arms. "We had a deal."

Walt snorted. "Hardly. I don't think—"

"OSCARRRRRR! WALLLLLLLTTT!" A voice came echoing from the vents. A few seconds later an enraged Wallace popped out from behind the sofa. He was dragging another rat behind him. A rat wearing a sailor shirt.

"LOOK!" Wallace made elaborate arm motions to show off the rat offender. "You'll never BELIEVE what I just found IN MY NEW APARTMENT!"

"Is it a rat?" Butterbean said. "I bet it's a rat."

"IT'S A RAT!" Wallace shrieked.

"See, I told you," Butterbean said proudly.

Wallace pushed the rat in the sailor shirt forward, like he was Exhibit A. "See? I found THIS GUY! Wearing MY CLOTHES! IN MY APARTMENT!"

Dunkin waved at the sailor-suit rat. "Hey, Ken."

Ken gave a short wave. "Hey."

"Wait, *your* clothes?" Marco said, frowning. "I'm pretty sure you were just borrowing those, right?"

"THAT'S NOT THE POINT," Wallace fumed. "I woke up to find THIS GUY . . ."

"Ken," Dunkin said.

"KEN!" Wallace corrected himself. "Trying on Mrs. Power Walker's tiny outfits. She almost WALKED IN ON HIM."

"Embarrassing," Dunkin smirked.

"You know it," Ken said.

"That's not the point." Wallace practically had smoke coming out of his ears. "Dunkin, are you TRYING to get us all kicked out? Because that's what's going to happen if they see you! And at this rate THEY'RE GOING TO SEE YOU!"

Dunkin shrugged. "Then I guess you'll have to work fast. Get us the loading dock back. Like you promised."

"We were supposed to start our annual bottle-cap shuffleboard tournament this week, but because of you guys, it's canceled," Lego said, nibbling on one of Butterbean's kibbles. "CANCELED. I was a top seed this year."

"Because of the raccoons, you mean," Marco said. "It's the raccoons' fault, not ours."

Dunkin shrugged. "Same difference." He strolled toward the kitchen. "Got any snacks?" He had made it as far as the dining room table when Mrs. Food's office door opened down the hall.

Oscar looked up at the clock. Mrs. Food was right on schedule. "SECOND CUP OF COFFEE!" Oscar crowed, jumping from one end of the perch to the other.

Wallace grabbed Ken by the shirtsleeve and shoved him behind the couch. Butterbean considered her options and then flopped down onto the rat named Lego. She was glad she had long hair. It made it harder to see his little arms sticking out from under her tummy.

Walt stalked slowly over to where Dunkin was standing, keeping her eyes on the approaching Mrs. Food.

"Don't move a muscle. You move, and it's all over," Walt hissed at him.

"Oh yeah? What'll you do?" Dunkin scoffed. "Turn me in?"

"No," Walt said, sitting down so that she loomed over him. "I'll catch you and give you to Mrs. Food as a gift. How does that sound?"

Dunkin went pale.

"That's what I thought," Walt said. She glanced over her shoulder to make sure she was blocking Dunkin from view, and then turned back and smiled down at him, displaying all of her teeth.

Dunkin didn't move.

Mrs. Food padded past them in her sock feet, humming as she went. The animals watched without moving as she poured herself another cup of coffee, and then padded back down the hallway to her office.

No one said a word until her office door had shut behind her again.

Then they sagged in relief.

"What are we going to do, Oscar?" Butterbean asked, standing up and helping a semi-squashed and disgruntled Lego to his feet.

"Emergency meeting." Oscar jumped to the end of his perch. "Rats, OUT. NOW. Stay in the vents if you have to, but no apartments. Apartments are OFF LIMITS. We'll be in touch soon." He pointed at the vent opening and kept pointing until the grumbling loading dock rats had all left the room.

Then he opened his cage door and landed in the

middle of the floor. "Okay, first things first. Wallace, we need to get that sailor shirt back before Mrs. Power Walker notices it's missing. Marco and Polo, we'll need to get Biscuit an update. As for the rest of us . . . whatever we have to do to keep those rats from being discovered, we do it. But first, we can forget about retirement. Officially."

"WHOOHOOO!" Marco jumped up doing a fist pump.

"So we're officially spies now? Officially official?" Polo clasped her hands together.

"Officially official," Oscar said grimly. "There's no going back now. Get ready for Operation Raccoon."

– 10 –

OPERATION RACCOON WAS OFF TO A ROCKY start.

The first thing Oscar had done was to send everyone out on secret reconnaissance missions. (Marco and Polo insisted that he call them reconnaissance missions instead of Oscar's preferred term, "things on their to-do list." Oscar's cage was also now known as Command Central.)

Marco and Polo's mission was to tell Biscuit what was happening. Wallace's mission was to try to get the sailor shirt back from Ken. Walt and Oscar were responsible for coming up with the actual details of Operation Raccoon. And Butterbean's mission was to provide cover for the rest of them by chewing the face off of her new squeaky lamb toy. She was very good at chewing the faces off of her toys.

So far the biggest problem with Operation Raccoon was that Walt and Oscar had no idea what the plan should be. Oscar had tried everything—staring at the ceiling, throwing fruit onto the floor, examining his feathers—but nothing had helped. He just didn't know what to do about the raccoon problem.

"Anything?" Walt said finally. She had spent her time pacing back and forth across the living room, hoping inspiration would strike. But it hadn't given her a single idea.

"Nothing," Oscar said, his feathers drooping. "What are we going to do?"

"Maybe it's not that big a deal," Butterbean said, spitting out a piece of cotton fluff. (Her mission was turning out to be a complete success.) "You told those rats to stay in the vents, right? I'm sure they'll listen to you."

"Maybe you're right," Oscar sighed. "They did seem to respect my natural leadership qualities."

"I hope so, because HOOOBOY is Biscuit mad," Marco said, crawling out from behind the sofa and brushing himself off. "We succeeded in our mission. We told him all about the raccoon situation."

"And we explained that you had a plan and it would be fixed in no time," Polo added, climbing out after Marco.

"But he's having a hard time keeping it together. He really wants to bark," Marco finished. "I mean, a LOT. He's just barely holding it in."

"He looked like he was going to explode," Polo said, making big explosion motions.

"I think his exact words were 'I can take them, let me at them, I'll rip them all to shreds,'" Marco said. "Then he shrieked into a couch pillow for five minutes straight."

"We had to help him take some deep cleansing breaths," Polo said. "He couldn't find a paper bag, though."

"I give him maybe a day before he snaps and starts barking again," Marco said.

"Totally." Polo nodded in agreement.

"Maybe I could talk to him again," Butterbean said, blowing a piece of fluff off her nose. "It helped last time."

"Maybe," Walt said, watching. She hated the idea of going back down to that apartment, but they might not have a choice. Butterbean may have totally misunderstood what therapy dogs did, but Walt had to admit she did have a calming effect on Second Floor Biscuit.

"Thanks for the report," Oscar said, watching Butterbean spit out another mouthful of fluff. (Butterbean's mission was maybe a little too successful. Someone was going to have a lot of cleaning up to do.)

"Did you happen to see Wallace while you were in the vents?" Walt asked.

"Yeah, he was right behind us." Marco leaned back toward the couch. "HEY WALLACE, TIME TO REPORT!" he yelled. "I think he had a rough time. He looked kind of messed up."

Wallace staggered out from behind the couch. Marco hadn't been kidding. Wallace's hair was sticking up in weird places, and he had a dazed expression on his face. He also had something orange and powdery on his hands and cheek that Butterbean was itching to sniff. She restrained herself.

"What happened to you?" Butterbean's nose quivered.

"That rat. Ken. That's what happened," Wallace said.

"You couldn't get the sailor shirt back?" Polo said sympathetically.

"No, I got it." Wallace grimaced. "He wasn't happy about it, but I got it."

"Did you have to go for the eyes?" Walt asked. (It was her number one recommended move.)

"No, nothing like that," Wallace said. "He'd just gotten some kind of powdery cheese dust all over the sleeve. I had to lick it off. It took a while."

"Erm. Good work," Oscar said, trying to ignore

the way his stomach turned over. He was not a fan of cheese dust. "Did you put the shirt back in Mrs. Power Walker's apartment?" He wasn't sure how clean it would look after having cheese dust licked off, but he wasn't going to be critical. It wasn't like Wallace had access to laundry facilities.

Wallace nodded. "I put it on the floor behind one of the chairs. It'll look like it fell off."

"Wow, that must've been a lot of licking," Marco said, eyeing the orange patch on Wallace's cheek. He loved powdery cheese dust. "Is that what you've been doing this whole time?"

"Not exactly." Wallace stared at the floor. "I, um. Well, I also moved out."

"Moved out?" Marco gasped. "From Mrs. Power Walker's apartment? But you just moved in!"

"You love Mrs. Power Walker's place!" Polo said.

"Think of the brownies!" Butterbean yelped.

Wallace shrugged. "I know, you're right. But I don't trust those rats not to come back. So I screwed the vent cover back on so they can't get in." Wallace looked pained. "It's just temporary. But I don't want to risk them sneaking in and messing things up for me."

"That's probably smart," Walt said, patting Wallace awkwardly on the head with one paw. She wasn't sure she trusted those loading dock rats either.

"You can stay with us, if you need to," Polo offered.

"Thanks. I checked all the vent openings to the other apartments," Wallace said. "Just to be sure. That's why I took so long. The basement vent's still open, but as far as I know, there's only one other apartment that's accessible by vent besides this one. And I don't think any rat would be stupid enough to sneak into that one."

"Oh really?" the white cat emerged from behind the sofa with a scrawny wriggling rat in her mouth. "Ptttppheewwww!" She spit the rat out onto the floor. It looked around wildly for a minute before spotting Walt and bolting back behind the sofa without a word. They could hear its footsteps echoing as it made its escape down the vent.

"I found that guy peeking into my living room while I was doing my warm-up dance routine," the white cat grumbled. "Groupies. My concentration was ruined."

"Who was THAT?" Butterbean gasped. "Did we know that one?"

Wallace shook his head. "I think that was Pocky? She's always been a snoop."

"Well, that's not good," Oscar said.

"No, it's not," the white cat said. "But trust me, we've got bigger problems now. Or rather, I have bigger problems right now." She sat down and took a deep breath. "Look, I hate to do this. But I need your help. I'm desperate."

Oscar blinked. He'd never seen the white cat look that way. "Of course. What's happened?" It had to be something bad if the white cat was asking for help. He braced himself. He didn't think he could take more terrible news right now. He was feeling a little overwhelmed, to be honest.

"Okay, thank you." The white cat looked relieved. "Wait here." She ducked behind the sofa and came out again carrying the bag of caviar treats she'd tried to give to Chad earlier.

"Now watch carefully," the white cat said.

Walt shot a skeptical look at Oscar, who shrugged.

"This is so exciting!" Butterbean whispered, watching the white cat intently. She had no idea what was going to happen.

The white cat slowly pawed a treat out of the bag, bent down, and popped it in her mouth. Then she started to chew.

Slowly her face contorted into a twisted grimace. Tears popped up in her eyes, and one eyelid started to twitch. Her nose started to dribble. She smacked her lips and then plastered a painful-looking smile on her face. "MMMMMMM," she purred. Then she turned and hacked violently behind the couch.

The animals looked at her in stunned silence.

"Um, what?" Walt finally said as the white cat reemerged, her eyes still watering. "What were we supposed to be watching, exactly?"

"THAT WAS SO EXCIT-ING!" Butterbean barked. "WHAT DID YOU EAT?"

The white cat sat down nervously and cleared her throat. "So. Give me your thoughts. Did I give the impression that the treats tasted . . ."

"Like vomit?" Polo said.

"Yes, absolutely."

"Terrible? Horrible? What's the word I'm looking for?" Marco tapped on his chin thoughtfully. "Repulsive? That one. Repulsive."

"Was it POISON?" Butterbean squealed. "Did I guess right?"

"GOOD! I was going for GOOD!" the white cat wailed. "It was supposed to look like a tasty treat."

"Um." Polo made a *yikes* face at Marco, who made one back.

"I'm guessing it was not convincing," the white cat said softly.

"In a word, no," Oscar said.

"Was that acting?" Walt said. "Because I don't think any of us were getting a 'good' vibe there."

The white cat slumped against the couch. "Oh misery! This is the worst thing that has ever happened to me! Even I, with my amazing talents, can't manage to make those disgusting treats look yummy. What am I going to DO? HELP ME!"

"But . . ." Polo looked confused. "Help you . . . how? Make them yummy?"

"Make them LOOK yummy," Marco whispered to Polo. "I think?"

Oscar cocked his head. "Wait, this is it? This is the big problem? This is what you think is worse than the raccoon situation?" Oscar jumped against the bars of his cage. "Cat, we've got real problems here!"

"MY PROBLEM IS REAL," the white cat wailed. "I CAN'T MAKE THOSE TREATS LOOK YUMMY! I'm a FAILURE."

Walt sniffed at the bag. "Cat, I don't think anybody can make those treats look yummy. They smell like sewage."

"I could lose my JOB!" The white cat moaned. "I have to eat these for a COMMERCIAL!"

Polo and Marco exchanged a significant glance. Then Polo stepped forward. "Um, I was just kidding earlier. Those looked DELICIOUS. Right, Marco?" She nudged Marco in the ribs with her elbow.

"Um. Yes, yum yum."

The white cat narrowed her eyes. "Really? I don't believe you."

"It's true. We were making a bad joke," Polo said, crossing her fingers behind her back. "Right, Walt? Because I was . . ."

"Jealous. We're just jealous of your success," Walt said in a flat voice. "Aren't we, Oscar? Tell the cat how good those treats looked."

"So good," Oscar said. "Now can we get back to the raccoons?"

The white cat sniffed. "I did try to make them look tasty. It's a hard job."

"Your performance was . . . stunning," Oscar said. "Indescribable. Really. We can help you practice more later if you want. But first, raccoons."

"Well, there are rats all over the vents," the white cat said. "So you'd better get that sorted out fast."

"Yes. Thanks for your input," Oscar said, clenching his beak. "Now, if you would just—"

He stopped midsentence. A key was turning in the lock. Madison.

"Get out! Go! You too, Wallace. She can't see either of you!" Walt hissed. Wallace ran for cover while the white cat rolled her eyes and sauntered behind the couch. She disappeared just as Madison opened the door.

"Madison . . ." Oscar said slowly. Then his face lit up. "Walt, that's it!" he crowed happily. "Madison's our solution."

Walt frowned in confusion. "Madison?"

Oscar hopped gleefully on his perch. "Of course! When she goes to the storage unit, maybe she'll see the raccoons! And if not, at least we'll get a status report. If we're lucky, we might not need to do anything. Heck, Bob might have already chased those raccoons away on his own."

"Maybe?" Walt said. She wasn't convinced. But at least they had a plan. Even if the plan was only waiting to see what Madison said.

Oscar nodded. "If I were a raccoon, I'd think twice about raiding Bob's building." He clicked his beak. "Let's make it official. Operation Raccoon is now Operation Wait and See."

Operation Wait and See took a lot longer than they'd expected.

Madison didn't seem to feel any urgent need to rush down to the storage area, no matter how many times Butterbean barked the words "storage area" at her. (And it was quite a few times. Oscar finally had to ask her to stop.)

She didn't go downstairs until after she and Mrs. Food had finished dinner.

"Oh shoot!" Madison said, making a face as she picked up pieces of squeaky-lamb fluff. "I'm sorry, I totally forgot to check the storage area. I'll go now."

"THANK YOU," Butterbean said. "FINALLY."

"You know the code?" Mrs. Food asked.

"Of course," Madison said, putting her shoes on. "I'll just be a sec."

"I'll go with her," Butterbean said, heading after her. But Madison was too quick for her. Butterbean almost got her nose caught in the door. (She had done that once and never wanted to do it again.)

Madison was back exactly seventeen minutes later. (Oscar had watched the clock. It was a very long seventeen minutes.)

"Anything missing?" Mrs. Food asked when she got back.

"Nope," Madison said, taking off her shoes and heading back to her room. "Everything looked just the same as always. There was just one unit that looked like it had been messed with. Probably the one that belongs to that lady on six. Ours looked fine."

"Well, that's a relief," Mrs. Food said, picking up her book. "I'll let Bob know tomorrow."

"Maybe the raccoons really did leave," Walt said

quietly after Mrs. Food had gone to bed. "Could it be that easy?"

"Bob probably scared them away," Butterbean said. Bob could be pretty intimidating sometimes.

"So Operation Wait and See continues," Oscar said.

"Operation Wait and See, Part Two," Butterbean said softly. She lay her head down on her feet. She had a lot of experience with waiting.

They didn't have to wait long.

The knock at the door came the next morning while Mrs. Food and Madison were eating breakfast.

Oscar dropped his piece of fruit onto the floor of his cage.

Butterbean dribbled kibble out of her mouth.

Walt looked up from her grooming in alarm.

"Well, here we go," Oscar said quietly. "The moment of truth."

Madison opened the door to find Bob standing in the hallway, solemnly holding his clipboard.

"Oh, um, hi," Madison said. "We checked the storage area, and everything looked good."

"Did it?" Bob said, taking a step inside. He didn't smile. "Because I checked this morning too. We've had another break-in. Vandalism. You know what vandalism is, Madison? Theft? Burglary?"

Oscar gripped his perch tighter. "Uh-oh." He shot Walt a panicked look. The raccoons were not gone. Operation Wait and See was turning into Operation Disaster.

"Um, yeah." Madison gave Bob a weird look.

"What's all this about, Bob?" Mrs. Food said, getting up from the table.

Bob smoothed the front of his shirt. "After we discovered the thefts this morning, we checked the security cameras. Looks like only one person went in last night. One." Bob tapped his clipboard against his hand. "Seems like we've got a pretty clear suspect."

"And who would that be, Bob?" Mrs. Food had a hard note in her voice.

Bob's face was grim. "Madison."

— 11 —

"I DID WHAT?" MADISON LOOKED OUTRAGED. "You think I vandalized the storage area?" She looked from Bob to Mrs. Food and back again.

"She did WHAT?" Butterbean yelped. "It wasn't Madison! It was the raccoons, right, Oscar?"

"Right," Oscar said in a low voice. "Oh, this is bad."

Mrs. Food put her hand on Madison's shoulder. "That's a very serious accusation, Bob."

Bob raised his hands defensively. "I don't like it any more than you do. But you can take a look at the surveillance video. Madison, you were the last one to go in last night. The ONLY one to go in. There was no damage before you went in. I had just checked it myself."

"But it wasn't me," Madison said. She turned to Mrs. Food, her voice pleading. "I didn't touch anything. I just went to our storage area. I told you, everything looked fine when I left."

"But can't they see it was the raccoons?" Butterbean whispered.

"Those cameras, they only show the humans—isn't that what Dunkin said?" Walt said softly. "They're positioned too high to show the floor."

"Right. And the raccoons wouldn't be coming in through the door." Oscar clicked his beak in frustration.

"I believe you, Madison," Mrs. Food said, shooting a steely glare at Bob. "Bob, this is a mistake. Madison didn't do this."

"I'd love to hear an alternate explanation. I really would. Madison?" He folded his arms and waited. "Can you explain this?"

Madison shifted from foot to foot. "No? I mean . . . I didn't . . ." Her chin started to quiver.

"Madison, why don't you finish getting ready for school while I talk to Bob," Mrs. Food said, patting Madison on the back. "I'll take care of this misunderstanding."

Madison nodded wordlessly and ran to her room.

Bob waited until Madison's door was shut before he turned back to Mrs. Food. "Look, there is nobody who wants this to go away more than I do. But the surveillance footage is pretty clear. It has to be Madison. And the sooner she comes clean, the better."

"She says she didn't do it, Bob." Mrs. Food's voice was hard. "I have to believe her. I'll want to see those surveillance tapes."

"Sure, sure." Bob rubbed his forehead. "And I admit, it's not like her. Maybe you'll see something I didn't. It's just that lady on six, she's on the condo board, and she's talking fines, disciplinary hearings, you name it. She's a real piece of work."

"Has she seen the tape yet?" Mrs. Food asked.

Bob shook his head. "Not yet. I've kept Madison's name out of it for now, but I won't be able to much longer."

Mrs. Food looked grim. "I'll be down to see the tapes right after Madison leaves for school."

Bob nodded and turned to leave.

"We've got to get those raccoons to stop!" Butterbean said after Bob had gone. "They're getting Madison in trouble!"

Oscar narrowed his eyes. "Oh, they'll stop. They'll have to. Or they'll have to deal with me."

Mrs. Food went downstairs to watch the surveillance tapes as soon as Madison left for school. Madison hadn't even said goodbye to the animals when she left. She had just stared at the floor and nodded whenever Mrs. Food tried to comfort her.

When Mrs. Food came back, she had Mrs. Third Floor with her. Mrs. Third Floor was Mrs. Food's best friend, and she said she was there for moral support. (Butterbean felt like that should be her department, since she was training to be a therapy dog, but she didn't say anything. Mrs. Food looked like she needed all the moral support she could get.)

"So if it wasn't Madison, who could it have been?" Mrs. Third Floor asked, sipping a cup of coffee. "There wasn't anyone else in the video?"

"No one," Mrs. Food said, frowning. "It was just like Bob said. No one went in after Madison. Not until Bob went in this morning."

"Aha!" Mrs. Third Floor said triumphantly. "Maybe it was Bob!"

Mrs. Food shook her head. "No, he barely comes into the room before he leaves again. You can see him reacting to the mess."

"Shoot," Mrs. Third Floor said, stirring her coffee. She stared into her cup.

"I don't see an explanation," Mrs. Food said.

"Could it be . . ." Mrs. Third Floor hesitated. "I mean, it couldn't be a ghost, could it?"

"NO!" Mrs. Food and Oscar and Walt burst out simultaneously. They'd already had to deal with Mrs. Third Floor imagining ghosts in the building. They didn't want to deal with that again.

"No, I don't think so," Mrs. Food said more calmly, patting Mrs. Third Floor's hand. "It is a mystery, though. I just wish I knew what to say to get Madison off the hook."

"Maybe you should talk to someone official? Maybe Carmen?" Mrs. Third Floor said tentatively. Carmen was a police officer who'd recently moved into the building. Butterbean's ears pricked up. Carmen had been helpful in their past investigations.

Mrs. Food shook her head. "She's out of town this week," she said. "And I really don't want to get the police involved if I can help it, even informally."

"That's understandable." Mrs. Third Floor sighed. "Well, we know Madison didn't do it. Maybe she can just lay low for a while, and it'll work itself out?"

"Maybe," Mrs. Food said. But she didn't sound convinced.

Walt was also not convinced. "That plan will absolutely not work," she said as they watched Mrs. Third Floor leave. "If some condo board member is out for blood, Madison won't be able to lay low enough. There won't *be* a low enough." She bristled at the thought. "Oscar, how soon can we activate Operation Raccoon?"

"Now," Oscar said, opening his cage door. "I'm going down now."

Walt blinked. "Um, hold on there a sec," she said, shooting a look in the direction of Mrs. Food. "How are you planning to do that? It's daytime. We can't just go down there, especially not if they're cleaning up the storage area. People will see us."

"I'm not going to the storage area," Oscar said calmly. "Here's the plan. Walt, you and Butterbean stay here. We need you to keep Mrs. Food occupied so she doesn't notice I'm gone. Marco and Polo—you head down into the vents. See if you can get information on what's going on in the storage area. I'll head down to talk to the raccoons."

Walt rolled her eyes. "Did you not hear me? The storage area has PEOPLE in it."

"That's not a problem," Oscar said, watching as Mrs. Food walked slowly down the hallway to her office. "Because I'm not going to the storage area. I'm going to the loading dock." He hopped out of his cage and flexed his wings. "Walt, open the window, please. I'm flying. OUTSIDE."

Operation Flying Outside (as Oscar was secretly calling it) took longer to implement than he'd expected.
About fifteen minutes longer, to be exact. Mostly
because he hadn't expected to spend fifteen minutes
arguing with Butterbean and Walt, who were convinced that his flying to the loading dock alone was a
bad idea.

Oscar was finally able to convince them they were
wrong. And now, seconds after leaping dramatically
out of the apartment window, he realized he'd been
right. It wasn't a bad idea.

It was a terrible idea.

Sure, launching himself out of the window had

felt heroic and exciting. But once Oscar was airborne, he was forced to admit a few uncomfortable truths. Namely, he was an apartment bird, and as an apartment bird, he was not in great flying shape. Also, he didn't know his way around outside very well. ("Very well" in this case meaning "at all.") And there were people. Lots of people. He could see them on the sidewalks, in cars, standing at bus stops, everywhere. Everywhere.

Oscar decided to ignore the people. (They were making him light-headed.) Instead, Oscar decided to focus on flying and keeping himself in the air. (Which was easier said than done.) He dove down a little lower and circled the building, scanning the ground for the loading dock. When he finally spotted it, he took one last backward glance in the direction of his window. He couldn't even tell which one it was anymore. Oscar didn't want to think about how he was going to find his way back.

Looking around anxiously, Oscar landed clumsily on the loading dock, trying hard to stay on his feet. His wings felt like jelly. And the last thing he wanted was to be seen by someone who knew about birds. Partly because a crash landing was always embarrassing, and partly because that someone would know that a mynah bird probably shouldn't be hanging out next to the building dumpster. (It was mostly the embarrassing part, though.)

But there was no one. Oscar breathed a sigh of relief, and then frowned. No people was a good thing. But no rats? No raccoons? That was a problem.

Oscar perched on the edge of the loading dock and peered down to the ground below. It was going to be very difficult to get the raccoons to stop if he couldn't find them.

Oscar cocked his head and examined the dumpster. If there was one place on this loading dock likely to attract raccoons, it had to be that dumpster. The lid looked like it was shut tight, but there was some intriguing-looking crud lying underneath on the ground. That had to be the spot.

Taking a deep breath, Oscar hopped off the loading dock. He just hoped he wasn't making the worst mistake of his life.

Marco and Polo hurried down the vents, their footsteps echoing as they went.

"We don't have Chad, so we won't be able to go into the storage room through the door," Marco said as he slid down one of the connecting vents.

"We'll just look through the grates. That's better

anyway," Polo said. "I don't want to accidentally run into Bob."

"Or a raccoon," Marco agreed. Polo shuddered. "So where should we start?" Marco asked. "Storage room or main basement area?"

"Basement?" Polo said.

"Right." Marco peered down a vent. "I think this is it?" The vents on the main floor weren't set up the same way as the upper-floor vents, since there were no apartments. "If we're lucky, maybe we'll find Dunkin or one of the other rats. We might not find them, though. Those guys can be pretty stealthy sometimes."

He slid down into the basement vent and then stopped short, blocking the vent opening. Polo slammed into him from behind, sending them both tumbling forward as she shot into the room.

"Hey!" Polo said. "What's the—oh. Guess we got lucky, huh?"

She stood up and looked around. The basement vent had basically become one long rat dormitory, with rats sprawled out on small white beds all along the walls. Polo examined the nearest bed. "Wait a minute! Is that a—"

"Pom-pom sock, that's right," Dunkin said, appearing out of the darkness. "Those are the best, see, because they have a built-in pillow."

"I know!" Polo said. She'd slept in a pom-pom sock once, and it really was comfortable. "Where'd you get them all?"

Dunkin looked shifty. "Oh, you know. Around."

"Um. Okay," Polo said, making a mental note to check Madison's sock drawer. "So what's going on down here? Any sign of the raccoons?"

Dunkin snorted. "Not hardly. They've taken over all of our best spots, and now the storage area isn't even safe. So this is what it's come to. Bunking in the vents." Dunkin made a face. "Did you know that maintenance guy has been in the storage area all day? Just because those raccoons had a party." He rolled his eyes.

"I know it seems bad," Polo said encouragingly. "But it's practically taken care of."

"Oscar's going to talk to the raccoons on the loading dock right now," Marco said. "He's got it covered."

"He was very determined," Polo said.

Dunkin snorted again. "Well, he'll have to get past that big one. The Raccoon King, I call him. He calls all the shots with those guys. And I don't think he's going to listen to any apartment bird. No offense." Dunkin shrugged. "Am I right, Ken?"

An arm shot up from the depths of one of the pom-pom socks and gave a thumbs-up. "Right," Ken's muffled voice called out.

Marco and Polo exchanged a worried glance. "Well, you don't know Oscar," Marco said.

"Yeah," Polo added. "One thing about Oscar. He knows what he's doing."

Oscar did not know what he was doing. It was insane, that's what it was. The patchy asphalt around the loading dock had gravel strewn around on it, and Oscar's feet made crunching sounds as he hopped awkwardly toward the dumpster. He was going to twist an ankle—he just knew it.

Taking one last look around to make sure the coast was clear, Oscar shaded his eyes and peered under the dumpster. There, in the shadows, he could see a dark pile, half-hidden by the dumpster wheels. It looked furry.

"Raccoons," Oscar said under his breath. He fluffed his feathers up to make himself look bigger, and then took one tentative step under the dumpster. The raccoons were asleep, which would make it easier to deal with them. He just needed to be firm. Stand tall. Tell them what's what. He could do that.

Taking a deep breath, Oscar marched over to the furry pile and nudged it with his foot. He braced himself, waiting. Then he nudged again.

Nothing.

Something was wrong. Oscar leaned over the fur pile, pushing it again with his foot. It felt wrong, somehow. Oscar cocked his head. It didn't just feel wrong. It SMELLED wrong. He peered closely at the pile and then gave a sharp barky laugh. It wasn't a pile of sleeping raccoons. It was a wadded-up fur coat.

Oscar felt himself deflate. He couldn't believe he'd been fooled like that. The coat smelled like flowery perfume and mothballs—it was obviously one of the items missing from the storage unit. He might not know everything about raccoons, but he knew enough to know that they didn't smell like flowers and mothballs. Oscar couldn't believe he'd wasted all this time for nothing.

He gave the coat one last frustrated kick, glaring at it as he did. He was just in time to see a pair of eyes gleaming in the darkness of the coat's folds.

And a hand reach out and grab his leg.

– 12 –

BUTTERBEAN AND WALT HAD THEIR DISTRAC-
tion techniques all planned out. Butterbean was going
with her signature move of running in circles and, in
case of emergency, the old standby, begging to go out.
Walt was planning to employ the sitting-on-Mrs.-
Food-so-she-couldn't-move technique, with her routine of coughing up a hairball as a last resort.

But as it turned out, it wasn't Mrs. Food they
needed to worry about. It was Madison.

"I'm HOME!" Madison yelled as she threw her book
bag into the apartment and kicked it across the floor.

"What?" Mrs. Food's surprised voice came from
the office.

"WHAT?" Butterbean yelped. She'd been dozing in the hallway, planning to cut Mrs. Food off at the pass at any sign of movement.

"WHAT?" Walt said, accidentally falling off the coffee table.

Madison wasn't supposed to be home for hours.

This was a disaster.

Walt stood up and shook herself off. Maybe things weren't that bad. Maybe it wasn't obvious that Oscar wasn't in his cage. Maybe no one would notice.

She looked back at Oscar's cage. The door was standing wide open, and it was perfectly obvious that a semi-large black bird wasn't sitting anywhere inside. Nope, definitely a disaster.

Mrs. Food opened her door and hurried down the hallway. "Madison? Why are you home so early?"

Madison kicked her book bag into its spot in the corner as she took off her jacket. "I told them I was sick and took the bus home." Mrs. Food looked shocked. "WHAT? I couldn't just SIT THERE with Bob thinking I'm some kind of criminal. I need to defend myself! I need to clear my name. I thought I'd go downstairs and do some investigating. Come on, Butterbean. Want to come?"

Butterbean wagged her tail. She absolutely wanted

to come. Especially if it would get Madison out of the house again.

Mrs. Food took Madison by the shoulders and steered her away from the front door. "That storage unit is the one place you are absolutely not going. You will stay as far away from there as possible until this is all cleared up. I'm working on it, but you need to leave this to me."

"But they think I'm a criminal!" Madison said.

"And we know you're not. And we'll prove it," Mrs. Food said, sitting Madison down on the couch.

"What do we do?" Butterbean moaned. She was standing in the middle of the living room, swaying back and forth. She didn't know if she should run, bark, or try to get outside. All of her distraction ideas were ruined.

"I don't know!" Walt said, hovering at the edge of the couch. "They haven't looked at the cage. Maybe they won't? I'm sitting on one of them—I don't care which one."

"Now, you're supposed to be sick? So be sick. Spend the afternoon watching bad TV. I'll make you some soup. Things will look better soon," Mrs. Food said, patting Madison on the shoulder and heading to the kitchen.

She didn't look at Oscar's cage.

"Madison it is," Walt said, pouncing onto Madison's

lap and kneading Madison's stomach before settling down for a long nap. "She won't move for hours."

Madison rubbed Walt on the head. "I didn't even say goodbye to you this morning," she said softly. "So I'll say hello now. Hello, cat!"

Walt purred in satisfaction. Madison wasn't going anywhere, not for a long time.

"Hello, Butterbean!" Madison called over to Butterbean, who was drooling uncontrollably. Anxiety made her spitty.

"Hi, rats," Madison called over to the aquarium.

"Oh no," Butterbean said. The rats weren't there. THE RATS WEREN'T THERE. She looked over at the rat cage. Marco and Polo had piled their cedar chips in one corner of the cage, so it looked kind of like they were sleeping. But only kind of.

Wallace peeked out from behind the couch. "Hey, guys! What's—"

"WALLACE!" Butterbean yelped. "Quick—GET IN THE RAT CAGE!"

"GO!" Walt said, leaning up and aggressively licking Madison's face. "She's not looking!"

Wallace didn't hesitate. He raced for the rat cage, climbed up the table leg, and leaped into the cage in record time. "I'm here!" he called, doing his best to look like two rats.

Butterbean sighed in relief. Disaster averted.

Walt stopped licking and curled back up, making herself as heavy as possible. Madison scratched Walt's neck again and then craned her neck around to look at Oscar.

"Hello, Oscar!" Madison called. Then she frowned. "Oscar?"

"Oh no," Walt said, twisting around and batting wildly at Madison's hair. Madison didn't pay any attention.

"WALT!" Butterbean barked. She started spinning in circles for a distraction, but Madison didn't even look at her.

Walt bumped Madison's chin with her head, but it was too little too late.

Madison sat up straight. "Oscar? OH NO!" She stood up, dumping Walt in a heap on the floor. "Mrs. Fudeker? Oscar's GONE!"

"So he's been doing this all day?" Polo said, pressing her face up to the grate. She was watching Bob clean up the storage area. He had the door to the basement elevator area propped open and was sweeping up what looked like confetti.

"Yup," Dunkin said, leaning against the wall.

"There's a lady that comes in every so often and yells at him. I think a lot of it's her stuff."

"The raccoons did all this?" Marco couldn't help but be impressed. They'd done some serious work in a short amount of time.

"Yeah, but don't forget, Madison's the one who's taking the blame." Polo's eyes narrowed. "As if Madison would go through people's storage units and throw their stuff around. Besides, she's just one kid! This took some time!"

"It's a lot easier when you've got a whole passel of raccoon friends to help out," Dunkin said. "Now, us rats, we would never do that. We're discreet. We never even use the storage area, except for our annual bottle-cap shuffleboard tournament. Which I guess is off this year. Thanks a lot, raccoons," he finished bitterly.

"That stinks," Marco said. He wasn't sure what shuffleboard was exactly, but it had to be exciting if there was a whole rat tournament.

"Yeah, tell me about it," Dunkin said. "I just feel bad for Ken. He's been champion four years running. This year was his chance to break the world record."

"Um. Sorry," Polo said, watching Bob drag a garbage bin across the storage room and open the loading dock door. "Well, I guess that's it, then? We should report back, Marco."

"Yeah, we should find out what Oscar—HOLY COW!" Marco pressed his face hard against the grate. "Did you see that? What was that?"

Just a few seconds after Bob opened the door to the loading dock, something large and black had flown at him, attacking his face and then flying across the storage room and into the basement.

"Was that—" Marco's mouth hung open as he stared wide-eyed at Polo.

"We have to go," Polo gasped. "WE HAVE TO GO NOW."

Oscar's life flashed before his eyes. "ACK!" he squawked, shaking his foot desperately. The hand tightened its grip.

"Oscar, isn't it?" a low voice growled. "So we meet again."

"Let go! Let go of my foot!" Oscar tugged against the hand holding on to his leg, but the grip was like steel.

"I don't know if you noticed, but I was asleep." The big raccoon poked his head out from underneath the folds of the coat. "I was asleep, and you kicked me. I don't like that, Oscar."

Oscar stopped shaking his leg and glared at the raccoon. (He wasn't going to get free anyway. He realized that now.) "You need to leave. You and the other raccoons, you're not welcome. I've warned you before. This is your last chance."

The raccoon laughed a cold laugh. "Leave? Or you'll do what? Who's the one who's trapped, bird? Not me."

"You're causing problems." Oscar tried to stand firm, but his other leg was shaking. "You don't want to make me angry," he said. He'd heard someone say something like that on the Television once, and it had been very effective.

Unfortunately it was less effective in real life.

"No, bird. You're the one who doesn't want to make ME angry. You're the one who needs to leave."

The raccoon loosened his grip on Oscar's leg and splayed his fingers wide in front of him. "I'm letting you go. But know this. If you or your friends ever bother us again, there will be serious consequences. Do not test me. You won't survive the test."

The raccoon disappeared back into the folds of the coat, leaving Oscar standing awkwardly a few paces away. Oscar took a deep breath. "You can't threaten—" he started.

And then the raccoon erupted out of the coat. "GO!" The raccoon snarled, teeth bared.

Oscar hopped backward, stumbling over a piece

of gravel and leaping into the air. The loading dock door opened, and Oscar saw his chance. He flew at top speed through the door, smacking into something in his way, and then streaked through the storage area and into the basement.

Oscar heard a commotion behind him, but he ignored it, pecking frantically at the elevator button.

The elevator dinged. Oscar flew inside, hovering near the ceiling as the elevator started moving. He just hoped he would be able to press the fourth-floor button before anyone else got on.

He wasn't that lucky.

"Lobby," the elevator voice said as the doors opened. An elderly woman stepped into the elevator and pressed the button for the seventh floor. And as the doors shut, she turned and looked up at the ceiling. Right at Oscar. He'd been seen.

She smiled at him. Oscar gasped in recognition.

It was Mrs. Power Walker.

Maintaining eye contact, she hovered her finger over the elevator button. "Three?" she said softly. "No? Eight? No. Four?"

Oscar squawked once. "Four it is!" Mrs. Power Walker said, smiling. Then she turned back to face the elevator doors.

Oscar landed on the railing inside the elevator

wall with a thump. His wings just weren't up to hovering anymore. Mrs. Power Walker didn't even seem to
notice. She didn't say another word until the elevator
opened on the fourth floor.

"Have a good day!" she called after Oscar as he flew
out into the hallway.

Oscar didn't think that was possible anymore.

"OH NO!" Madison ran around the apartment, looking at the tops of all of the bookcases and cabinets.
"He's not anywhere. How could he get out?"

Mrs. Food was in the living room, looking behind
couch cushions. "I'm sure he's fine. He's probably just
hiding."

"Oh, this is bad," Butterbean said as she tailed Madison around the apartment. "We messed up distracting, Walt!"

"I should've gone for the hairball," Walt said. "It never fails."

"I should've peed on the rug! Why didn't I pee on the rug?" Butterbean wailed.

"Maybe he's in one of the bedrooms?" Mrs. Food said, putting back the last couch pillow.

"Good idea!" Madison ran down the hallway, with Mrs. Food close behind her.

"Holy cow, you guys! You are not going to believe—" Marco yelled as he and Polo came streaking out from behind the couch. Marco held up one finger as he bent over panting. It was a lot farther from the basement to the fourth floor than he'd thought. "You are not going to BELIEVE—" he started again.

"Get in the cage! GET IN THE CAGE!" Walt said, running over and nudging Marco toward the rat cage. "You too, Polo. RUN!"

"Emergency situation!" Butterbean explained as she raced by. (She was doing her circles again. It might not have worked as a distraction, but it worked as a freak-out technique.)

Marco and Polo scrambled up the table legs and belly flopped into their cage just as Madison came back into the room. She looked around aimlessly and then gasped.

"OH NO!" Madison said, pointing at the open window. She turned to Mrs. Food, her eyes wide. "Do you think he got outside?"

"Oh no, no, he wouldn't do that," Mrs. Food said. But she had gone pale.

"But he's not ANYWHERE," Madison said, on the verge of tears. "We'll never find him! It's all my fault!"

"How is it HER fault?" Butterbean asked.

"Beats me," Walt said. "It's obviously my fault."

"It's the raccoons' fault," Butterbean said.

Madison peered out of the window. "I don't see him. If he got out, he's just GONE."

"Have you checked the hallway? Maybe he got out there somehow?" Mrs. Food said, trying to sound hopeful. But she couldn't take her eyes off of the open window.

"Good idea, maybe he's there," Madison said, her voice thick. She wiped her eyes and then hurried to the front door.

"Oscar?" she called as she threw the door open wide. And was immediately hit in the face by a large mynah bird streaking into the room.

"OOF!" Madison said. "Oscar?"

"Why do I keep doing that?" Oscar wailed. "Excuse

me! Apologies!" he called over his shoulder as he flew over to his cage. He crash-landed inside, collapsing on the floor with his wings stretched out. They were quivering with exertion. Oscar hoped they'd recover. "I'm back," he croaked.

"He's back!" Madison cheered. "How did he get out?"

"I must've forgotten to close the door to his cage," Mrs. Food said, hurrying over to the cage and closing the door. "I am so sorry, Oscar." She turned to Madison. "He looks traumatized, poor guy. I wonder how long he was out there?"

"Too long," Oscar said softly.

"Thank goodness he's back," Madison said, sinking down on the couch. "We found him."

"Thank goodness you were here," Mrs. Food said, sitting down next to her. "See? It turned out all right in the end."

Madison nodded.

Oscar looked down at Walt and Butterbean. "I failed. This isn't going to turn out all right. The raccoons aren't leaving."

Butterbean nodded. "It's okay," she said. "We failed too."

Walt sat down, her face grim. "You didn't fail, Oscar. None of us did. We just haven't succeeded." She curled her tail around her feet. "Yet."

– 13 –

"You hit Bob in the face?" Butterbean couldn't believe it. She'd never even considered something like that, and she and Bob had had some issues.

Oscar cringed. "It was an accident," he said for the third time. He hadn't even realized it had been Bob at first—Bob had just been an obstacle to deal with as he was making his escape from the raccoon. Oscar had been so relieved to see that door open, he hadn't stopped to consider why it had opened. Or who had opened it. Or that Oscar might want to take evasive maneuvers when he flew inside. It was just the shortest way to get home again (and the only way he thought his wings could handle). Oscar made a mental note to do some more wing exercises in the future. (And to look where he was going.)

"But the FACE!" Butterbean said again. "And then Madison's face! So many faces!" She couldn't get over it. As far as she could remember, Oscar had never hit ANYONE in the face before, and now here he was with two in one day! It was definitely a day to remember.

"Again, accident," Oscar said. "Not something I'd recommend." He cleared his throat. "Now, we need to get down to business. Plan out Operation Raccoon, um, Part Two."

"Right. We need to figure out what to do next," Walt said. "Any ideas?"

"Isn't it obvious?" Butterbean asked. "Forget Operation Raccoon, Part Two. It's time for Operation Dog Therapy. I've got to go down there."

Walt took a deep breath. "No, Butterbean. You can't go down there. How many times do we have to tell you? Therapy dogs and therapists are not the same thing!"

Polo raised her hand tentatively. "It's true, Butterbean. I've seen shows on TV with therapists. I don't think any of them are dogs."

She looked at Marco for confirmation. He nodded. "She's right. No dogs."

"It's true. They're mostly people," Wallace agreed.

"Besides, therapists are licensed professionals," Walt said. "You know how important licenses are, don't you?"

Butterbean looked down at her dog tag. "Yes," she grumbled. "But . . ." She looked around the group. "But Madison said I'd be a great therapist."

"Maybe you would," Oscar said. "But it's not safe, Butterbean." He hopped farther down the perch to be nearer to Butterbean. "Those raccoons aren't playing around. That big raccoon, he threatened us. We need to be stealthy. Going down there like I did was a mistake. I was lucky to escape."

"Besides, thanks to Oscar, Madison and Mrs. Food are going to be watching us all like hawks," Polo said. "No offense, Oscar."

"None taken," Oscar said grimly. He knew it was true. Now that they knew he could get out, he didn't know what was likely to happen.

"So, what are we going to do?" Marco said finally.

"We'll figure it out," Walt said. She flattened her ears as Madison came into the room. "Later. We'll figure it out later."

Madison came over and sat down on the floor next to Butterbean, rubbing her ears sadly. "I can't even investigate, Bean. They won't let me do anything."

Butterbean leaned heavily against Madison's leg. "Tell me about it."

"I know, I know," Madison said. "Mrs. Fudeker said she'd handle it. But I'd feel better if we could go down there and see for ourselves. Do a stakeout, like we did with that apartment on the fifth floor! We'd have it solved in no time."

"We're working on it, Madison," Butterbean wuffled softly. "We'll clear your name."

"You'll help too, won't you, Bean? You'll keep an eye out for me?" Madison asked.

"Of course I will," Butterbean said, leaning her head against Madison's. "Didn't I just say that?" she whispered to Walt. Walt shrugged.

Madison smiled and hugged Butterbean. "You crazy dog. I know you can't do anything, but you make me

feel better." She smiled a watery smile and scrambled to her feet. "Good night, you guys," she said to the animals as she turned and went down the hall to her bedroom.

Butterbean beamed at Walt. "See? What did I tell you? I'm a terrific therapist."

Since Madison had gone to bed early (after wandering around grousing about how unfair it was that she couldn't go investigate herself), the animals hoped they'd have a chance to make a new plan. But no such luck. Mrs. Food didn't seem like she had any intention of going to bed. After Madison went to her room, Mrs. Food picked up her book and started reading. And reading. And reading some more.

"HOW LONG IS THAT BOOK?" Butterbean whined, watching Mrs. Food read. (It was less exciting than it sounded.) "What are we going to do?"

Mrs. Food smiled at her. "Shh, Butterbean. It's bedtime." Then she went back to her book.

"How are we supposed to plan with her here? She keeps shushing me!" Butterbean complained in a spitty whisper.

Oscar adjusted his feathers. "We may not be able to take any action tonight. But that might be a good thing. I have to admit, I'm at a loss as to what we should do."

"Oscar? Quiet down now," Mrs. Food said without looking up.

Oscar clicked his beak in frustration. "We'll reassess the situation in the morning," he whispered, keeping one eye on Mrs. Food. "Come at them when they don't expect it. Sound good?"

"But we need to do something NOW!" Butterbean whimpered softly.

Walt stalked over to Mrs. Food and sat down, waiting to be petted. Mrs. Food patted her once on the head absentmindedly and then went back to her book. Walt shook her head. "She's not going anywhere, folks."

"That settles it. Early night for everyone, and we'll reconvene in the morning," Oscar said, fluffing up his feathers. He tucked his head under his wing. To be honest, he hadn't been looking forward to a long night of planning. It really had been an exhausting day.

"If you say so," Marco said, stifling a yawn. "Me, I could plan all night, but sleeping on it might be a good idea."

"Sounds good to me," Polo said, burrowing into a pile of cedar chips.

"Wallace, we'll be starting early tomorrow, so you'll want to stay here," Oscar said sleepily.

"If you insist," Wallace said, snuggling down into the cedar chips in the corner of the cage. It was nice to have a sleepover, now that his apartment was off limits.

"But . . . that's not . . . We should . . ." Butterbean said, veering back and forth between the birdcage and the rat cage. She turned to Walt. "Walt, shouldn't we do something? What about Biscuit? What about the raccoons?"

Walt sighed. "Mrs. Food is awake and RIGHT THERE. Even if we had a plan, WHICH WE DON'T, we couldn't do it until really late." She patted Butterbean on the back. "Oscar is right. We need sleep. We'll figure out what to do in the morning."

Walt curled up in her bed and closed her eyes. Then she opened them again. "Butterbean? Go to sleep."

"But . . ." Butterbean wuffled, looking around the

room and wandering aimlessly for a few minutes. They were right. There was nothing she could do. But doing nothing just felt wrong. Butterbean lay down behind Madison's book bag on the floor. She might not be able to do anything, but she'd be ready for the morning. She closed her eyes.

A sharp tap on the door startled them open again. Butterbean's head jerked up. She looked from the door to Mrs. Food. Mrs. Food looked as surprised as she was.

"What on earth?" Mrs. Food checked her watch and put down her book. The tapping came again.

"Wha—" Oscar untucked his head and looked around. "What's going on?"

Walt opened one eye. "Huh?" She wasn't prepared to open the other one unless it was something important.

Mrs. Food hurried over to the door and peered out through the peephole. She muttered angrily to herself.

She took a deep breath and pulled the door open. "Harriet." Her voice was flat.

Butterbean peeked around her legs. Mrs. Food didn't even notice her. Butterbean looked out into the hallway. Mrs. Hates Dogs on Six was standing there, her arms folded. "Beulah."

"It's very late, Harriet," Mrs. Food said stonily. "Can I help you with something?"

"I'm here about that juvenile delinquent living with you," Mrs. Hates Dogs on Six said, curling her lip like the words left a bad taste in her mouth. "I know she's the one who destroyed and stole my valuables. I know she vandalized the storage room. And I'm here to let you know that she's not getting away with it. If Bob and the management don't take action, I will. I will be calling the police and having that child ARRESTED. And you will be EVICTED, do you hear me? EVICTED."

"I have to do something," Butterbean said under her breath. Mrs. Hates Dogs on Six couldn't evict Madison and Mrs. Food! And Madison in jail? Butterbean couldn't let that happen.

Mrs. Food set her jaw. "Good night, Harriet." She started to close the door, but Mrs. Hates Dogs on Six reached out and stopped it.

"Did you hear what I said?" Mrs. Hates Dogs on Six demanded.

"I'll be back, you guys," Butterbean said softly, looking over her shoulder at Walt.

"Butterbean, no," Walt said, sitting up abruptly.

Butterbean eyed the partially open door. She tentatively reached out and put one paw into the hallway. Then she looked up at Mrs. Food and Mrs. Hates Dogs on Six. They were locked in a stony staring contest. It was her one chance.

Butterbean gritted her teeth and quietly slipped out between Mrs. Hates Dogs on Six's legs. No one noticed. No one except for Walt and Oscar.

"BUTTERBEAN!" Oscar squawked, throwing himself against the side of his cage. "STOP!"

"Did you hear me?" Mrs. Hates Dogs on Six asked again. "Jail, Beulah. That's where that criminal is going," Mrs. Hates Dogs on Six smirked. "And there's nothing you can do to stop it."

"OH NO YOU DON'T," Walt said, streaking across the room.

Mrs. Food leaned down and intercepted Walt just as she reached the door. And when she stood up again, her face was calm and unconcerned.

"I understand you're upset, Harriet, but Madison is not the one responsible," Mrs. Food said quietly. "And it's far too late for me to listen to your threats. Good night."

She closed the door firmly in Mrs. Hates Dogs on Six's face. Then she locked the door and leaned back against it, breathing heavily. She pressed her face into Walt's fur.

"That woman," she said shakily. "I'm just glad Madison wasn't awake to hear that." She set Walt down onto the floor. "I'm too angry to read anymore. Time for bed."

"But BUTTERBEAN!" Walt wailed, jumping up against Mrs. Food's legs, and then turning and pawing at the door.

"BUTTERBEAN GOT OUT!" Oscar shrieked, flapping his wings against the side of the cage. "THE RACCOONS!"

Mrs. Food looked over at Oscar. "Oh, you poor thing. You've had such a scary day. And I know that woman didn't help matters." She walked over to his cage and touched the bars lightly. "Sounds like you could use your cover tonight."

"What?" Oscar's eyes got wide. "NO! NOT THE COVER!"

Mrs. Food picked up a quilted cage cover and put

it over Oscar's cage. "Good night, Oscar," she said softly, fastening the corner of the cover so it wouldn't come off. And so the cage door wouldn't open.

"NO!" Oscar's voice became muffled.

Mrs. Food patted the top of the cage and looked down at Walt. "Come on, you. I could use a little company tonight."

Walt shrunk back. "No, I've got to get Butterbean!" Mrs. Food picked Walt up and carried her off down the hall. "She's in danger!" Walt yowled.

She stared back into the living room, her face panicked. "Marco! Polo! Butterbean got out! Wallace, wake up! You've got to stop her!"

Marco flopped over onto his back and let out a loud snore.

"Popcorn," Polo muttered in her sleep before snuggling back down into the cedar chips.

"BUTTERBEAN!" Walt cried one last time as Mrs. Food closed the door to her room.

The living room was almost silent. The only sound was of three rats sleeping, and a muffled rattling from the birdcage in the corner.

– 14 –

BUTTERBEAN DUCKED BEHIND A SUPPORT
beam in the hallway. She watched as Mrs. Food shut
the door on Mrs. Hates Dogs on Six. And she watched
as Mrs. Hates Dogs on Six stormed down the hallway,
pushing the elevator button so many times and so
hard that Butterbean was surprised that she hadn't
hurt her finger.

Butterbean waited until the elevator came and she
was sure that Mrs. Hates Dogs on Six had left. Then
she poked her head out and looked around.

The hallway was empty.

To be honest, Butterbean never really thought
she'd be able to sneak past Mrs. Food. And even then,

she expected Mrs. Food to come out looking for her right away. But it didn't look like anyone had missed her. It gave Butterbean a queasy feeling in her stomach.

She stepped out into the hallway and glanced back at Mrs. Food's door. They hadn't missed her YET. She didn't have much time.

Butterbean trotted down the hallway and pushed the button to the elevator. (It was hard not to do her jaunty walk, because even though everything was very serious, she was still OUTSIDE THE APARTMENT. BY HERSELF. In the hallway without even her LEASH.)

Butterbean pushed the elevator button again, in case that would help. (Mrs. Hates Dogs on Six had seemed to think it would.) Then she waited anxiously, shooting looks back at Mrs. Food's door every few seconds.

She knew what she needed to do. She just couldn't get caught. Her plan would work.

The elevator dinged. The doors opened. It was empty.

So far so good.

Butterbean straightened herself up to full height (which, to be fair, wasn't very tall) and marched inside. Operation Dog Therapy had started.

Walt paced around the bedroom, her tail twitching anxiously. Butterbean was gone. Probably in trouble. And there wasn't anything Walt could do.

Mrs. Food hadn't even really needed company. She'd just patted Walt on the head a few times and climbed into bed, falling asleep almost right away. She was already snoring.

Walt circled the room one more time. Before the knock on the door, Walt had barely been able to keep her eyes open, but now she didn't think she was ever going to sleep again.

Walt sat down and looked around, a sinking feeling in her stomach. She'd been so careful to make a secret escape route behind the couch in the living room. She could go anywhere, at any time, and no one would ever know.

She'd thought she'd been so smart. It had never occurred to her that she might need one in the bedroom. But she did. And now it was too late.

She was trapped.

Oscar stared at the flowery quilted cover surrounding his cage. It had always made him feel cozy before, but now it just made him feel claustrophobic. He cocked his head and listened as hard as he could, but he couldn't tell what was going on in the living room. He didn't even know if anyone was in there. It was like he was sitting in a soundproof box. Anything could be happening out there. Anything.

Oscar dumped his food dish out onto the floor in disgust. He was useless. He should've taken Butterbean's therapy talk more seriously. But he hadn't. And now she was in danger.

Marco's feet twitched in his sleep, like he was running in a dream. (He was.) He kicked one of his hind feet out hard, hitting Polo squarely on the head. She sat up abruptly and looked around, her eyes bleary. She stared for a long minute at Oscar's covered cage, frowning. Then she blinked and swayed slightly. She blinked again, but this time her eyes stayed shut. "Celery sticks," she murmured as she stretched out onto her stomach and fell back asleep.

"Mmmmm," Wallace muttered to himself in his sleep. He'd always loved celery sticks.

Walt was tired of pacing. She was tired of staring at the clock. She wasn't even sure how long it had been. Maybe minutes. Maybe hours. (Standard clocks were still a mystery to her.) But she knew one thing. She wasn't waiting anymore.

"OUT! NOW! MRS. FOOD!" Walt yowled from her position at the door. Mrs. Food's only response was a soft snore.

Walt jumped up onto the bed to assess the situation. Mrs. Food was lying on her back with her mouth open slightly. Walt examined her carefully. Definitely asleep. She leaned over and meowed loudly into Mrs. Food's ear. No reaction.

"Ahem. Mrs. Food?" Walt meowed again, batting Mrs. Food on the nose with one paw.

Nothing.

Walt batted again, on Mrs. Food's chin this time. Mrs. Food stayed asleep. (Although Walt suspected she might be faking.)

Walt shook her head. She had no choice. She was going to have to go big. She just hoped Mrs. Food would understand.

Standing up, Walt stepped heavily onto Mrs. Food's stomach.

"OOF!" Mrs. Food let out a puff of air, but her eyes were still closed.

Walt walked slowly up to Mrs. Food's head. Then, turning around, she lay down squarely on Mrs. Food's face.

"MMMFFFRTTTH . . ." Mrs. Food sputtered, spitting cat fur out of her mouth. "Wha . . ." She sat up, pushing Walt onto the pillow. "That's it, cat," she said, flinging the covers back and staggering to her feet. Then she marched over to the bedroom door, throwing it open wide. "Out!"

Walt didn't need to be asked twice. Without a backward glance, she streaked out of the room and disappeared down the hallway.

"Hello? Is someone there?" Oscar cocked his head. He couldn't be sure, but it looked like the cover on his cage had shifted a little. He shifted on the perch and cocked his head to the other side. "Hello? Is someone—WHOOOOOAAA!" Oscar clung to his perch as something landed with a thud on top of his cage, making it swing violently from side to side.

Oscar tumbled to the floor of his cage. He'd only ever had this happen once before, and that had been a few years earlier when a delivery man had knocked his cage over by mistake. (Oscar had dubbed it the Great Cage Catastrophe. It still gave him nightmares.) He squeezed his eyes shut and braced himself for impact.

But the crash didn't come.

Instead, there was a slippery sliding noise as the

quilted cover fell to the floor, making the cage swing even more crazily.

Oscar wobbled over to the bars to peer out.

There, on the floor, was Walt. She was sprawled in a heap with the cage cover tangled around her. She stood up and shook herself off, stepping gracefully out of the crumpled fabric.

"Well? What are you waiting for?" Walt demanded, smoothing her fur. "Butterbean's in trouble. Let's go."

Walt and Oscar made it down to the basement in record time. They hadn't even waited to make sure that no one was in the elevator—they just bolted inside as soon as the doors opened. (Luckily it was empty.) But aside from a few signs of Butterbean here and there (a patch of drool by the elevator doors, a clump of hair stuck to the elevator rug), there was no sign of the dog herself.

"We'll get there in time," Oscar said quietly, watching the numbers light up. "She's fine." But his words sounded hollow. They both knew that might not be true.

"That raccoon wasn't joking," Walt said in a low voice. "That threat was real."

Oscar didn't say anything. They both knew Walt was right.

"Basement," the elevator voice said. Walt leaned against the doors, and as soon as they opened, she raced out of the elevator. Three rats were standing outside the door to the storage area.

One stepped forward, holding his hands up defensively. "We tried to stop her. Don't blame us."

"She wouldn't listen," the second rat said, wringing her hands.

Walt and Oscar looked at each other in dismay.

"Um. Thanks . . . Pocky, was it?" Oscar said.

"I'm Lego," the first rat said. "That's Pocky." He jerked his head toward the second rat. "And over there, that's Ken."

"Hey," the third rat said, lifting his hand in a low wave. "Your dog friend? She's in there. It's been a while."

"Yeah. You shouldn't go in there," Lego said. "It's bad."

"Is she really a therapist?" Pocky asked.

"But how did she get in?" Walt asked. That had been the one thing giving her hope. That Butterbean wouldn't be able to get inside. She couldn't go through the vents, after all, and no one was with her to open the door. She turned on Pocky, the rat who was closest to her. "Was it you? Did you open the door for her?"

"Not us," Pocky said, raising her hands up. "Him." She jerked her thumb upward.

Chad, dangling from the exit sign, waved a tentacle. "How's it going?"

"Chad?" Oscar couldn't believe it. It had never occurred to him that Butterbean might have an accomplice.

"Why would you do that?" Walt demanded.

"What? She showed up at my door. She said she'd pay. Canned tuna," Chad said grouchily. "How was I supposed to know this was a rogue operation?"

"We have to go in there. Now." Oscar nodded toward the door.

"I CAN'T SAY NO TO CANNED TUNA!" Chad said, waving his free tentacles wildly.

Walt glared at him. "Just open it, Chad."

"Sure, no problem. I'm just the doorman," Chad grumbled. "You know me, I live to open doors." He pushed the key code and glared at them. "And just so you know, I was BEING HELPFUL. This is NOT MY FAULT."

Chad snorted huffily as he tugged at the handle with one of his free tentacles. The door swung open.

Walt and Oscar squeezed through the gap and then stopped short, their eyes wide. It was worse than they'd thought.

— 15 —

BUTTERBEAN WAS SURROUNDED. THE RACCOONS were pressed in so close around her that Walt and Oscar could only see the top of her head. Oscar swallowed hard. There were so many raccoons. But strangely, they didn't even seem to notice Walt and Oscar.

"Butterbean!" Oscar croaked as he and Walt pushed through the wall of raccoons. It didn't matter how many there were. They had to get to Butterbean. They had to save her.

Walt ducked under tails and around raccoon armpits as she made her way into the circle, followed quickly by Oscar. But whatever they'd expected to see, this was not it.

"Butterbean?" Walt said in a hushed voice.

"Shh!" Butterbean said, frowning at them. She was sitting on a thin pillow in the center of the circle, right next to an ordinary cardboard box. Walt blinked. A cardboard box that had the big raccoon lying on top of it. Butterbean shot Walt and Oscar another stern look and then turned to the raccoon. "I'm sorry. Go on."

"It's just . . . do you know what they call us?" the raccoon said, a tear trickling down his cheek. Oscar couldn't believe it. He didn't sound anything like the scary raccoon he'd been earlier. But it was definitely the same one. "Do you? They call us . . . they call us . . ."

"You're in a safe space," Butterbean said, patting him on the shoulder.

"TRASH PANDAS!" The raccoon sniffled. "They call us trash pandas!"

"Oooooohhhhhhhh," the crowd of raccoons murmured.

"And how does that make you feel?" Butterbean asked.

"Terrible! It feels horrible," the big raccoon said. "Why would they say that?"

Loud sniffles came from the raccoons in the circle. It was obviously an emotional moment for all of them. Oscar edged closer to Walt. He'd never called a raccoon a trash panda in his life, but he still felt guilty somehow.

"You know you're not a trash panda," Butterbean said quietly. "Pandas are bears. I've seen them on the Television."

"Right?" the raccoon said. "It's not even ACCURATE. It's so wrong!"

Oscar cleared his throat. "Um, Butterbean?"

"Oscar?" Butterbean said softly. "Could this wait until the session is over?"

"Um, sure, no problem," Oscar said awkwardly. "We'll be, um . . . over there?" He waved vaguely in the direction of the door. He didn't think he had it in him to be more specific.

"Good, that's fine. The hour is almost up," Butterbean said calmly. She turned back to the raccoon. "Now. Tell me about your mother."

Walt and Oscar sat on the floor next to the door, with Chad dangling over their heads, staring blankly into the room. It was a lot to take in.

"How many therapy shows does Butterbean watch?" Walt finally asked.

Oscar shook his head. Obviously way more than he'd realized.

"I hear she's very affordable," a small raccoon in a sequined tube top said in a low voice, sidling up to Oscar. "Although it's hard to get an appointment."

"You don't say," Oscar said. The whole thing was like a dream. He wished he could pinch himself to see if he was awake, but wings weren't great for pinching.

"That's it. My tentacles are getting crispy," Chad said, dropping to the floor. "If you need me, I'll be in the utility sink." He scooted across the floor, around a pair of raccoons playing with croquet mallets, and climbed up into the sink. "Step aside, bub," he said to a raccoon who was carefully washing a shiny harmonica.

Butterbean's therapy session seemed to be ending. The big raccoon patted her on the back a few times and gave her an awkward hug. Then he turned and looked over at Oscar. They locked eyes, and after a second the big raccoon raised his hand in a half salute. Oscar blinked. This could not be happening.

Butterbean trotted over. "Hey, guys, did you see?

I did a whole therapy! I knew I'd be great at it. Reginald said I really helped him work through some things."

"Reginald?" Walt stared at Butterbean like she'd never seen her before.

"You know, the big raccoon over there. He says he knows you, Oscar," Butterbean said. She looked over her shoulder at the big raccoon. "REGINALD! Come say hi to my friends!" She turned back to Oscar. "Is he the one who threatened you?"

"Urk," Oscar said as Reginald the big raccoon lumbered over and stood looming over them.

"Reginald, you know Oscar, and this is Walt," Butterbean said. "I think you have something to say to Oscar?"

Reginald grimaced. "Yeah. Um. About that. I said some stuff earlier, and . . . I shouldn't have." He punched Oscar lightly on the shoulder. (Not as lightly as Oscar would've liked, though. He almost knocked him over.) "No hard feelings?"

"Um, no, none at all," Oscar said, fluffing his feathers, doing his best to look calm and collected. "We both said things we shouldn't have." Although, to be fair, Oscar didn't recall grabbing anyone by the foot.

"I told Reginald about Madison and the 'situation,'" Butterbean said, making clumsy air quotes.

"And about that dog's bangs," Reginald said, his eyebrows shooting up. "That's a tough break."

"And?" Walt said suspiciously. Sure, he seemed friendly now, but Walt still wasn't sure she trusted this Reginald character.

Reginald folded his arms. "And I'm in. We'll do whatever you need. What can we do to help?"

Marco opened his eyes. He had the distinct feeling that someone was staring at him. It had messed up his dream. (Which was a particularly good one too, involving a mountain of popcorn.)

He sat up and immediately let out a scream.

"WHA? What is it?" Polo said, jerking upright into a sitting position. Then she stifled a scream too.

The white cat had her face pressed up against the side of the rat's aquarium and was silently watching them.

"Don't DO that!" Polo squealed, getting up and stomping over to the water bottle to climb up.

"I wondered how long it would take you," the white cat said, smirking. "You have NO IDEA how long I was here."

"Ha-ha, very funny. Good joke," Marco said shakily. An enormous cat face was not the way he liked to wake up in the morning. Although, looking around, he wasn't sure it was morning. It still looked like night to him.

"Cat treat?" The white cat nodded toward the package of caviar treats on the counter.

"For the last time, no." Polo made a face. "Those things are disgusting."

"I know," the white cat said sadly. "So, where is everyone? I thought with everything going on, you'd at least be planning some daring escapade. No plans for a late-night confrontation?"

"What do you mean, where is everyone? We're right here," Polo said. "HEY, WALLACE," she called down. "Wake up!" She turned back to the white cat. "See, there's Wallace. All accounted for."

The white cat gave her a pitying glance. "All accounted for except for one bird, one dog, and one black cat. Any idea where they might be?"

Polo's eyes got wide. "Oh no." She looked down at Marco and Wallace. "They're not here?"

The white cat stood back so they could see the living room. "Do you see anyone else?"

The white cat was right. The room was empty. And Polo could just make out a piece of orange paper that had been slipped in between the door and the frame. The piece of paper they used when they needed to sneak out.

"OH NO!" Polo turned to Marco, her eyes huge.

"Basement?" Marco said, climbing out of the cage.

Polo nodded. "BASEMENT! NOW!"

"No way. Forget it," Reginald said, his face stony. "Absolutely not."

Oscar reeled back a little. They'd gone from "whatever you need" to "no" in record time. He should've known it wouldn't be that easy.

"Why not?" Walt said, lashing her tail.

"What's wrong with the plan?" Butterbean asked.

"What's WRONG WITH IT?" Reginald demanded. "You want us to GET CAUGHT!"

"Well," Butterbean said. "Just a little."

"And not really CAUGHT caught," Walt said.

"We just need them to know that Madison's not the one doing this," Oscar clarified. "That's all. We don't want them to actually catch you."

Reginald glared at them, his eyes cold. "Look, I've got a soft heart. I don't want the kid to go to jail. But do you KNOW what they do to raccoons that get caught?"

Oscar shifted uncomfortably. "Um. Not exactly."

"ME NEITHER," Reginald boomed. He seemed 100 percent back to his old intimidating self. "And I DON'T WANT TO FIND OUT."

"Urk." Oscar swallowed hard.

"That goes for these guys too," Reginald said, waving

his arm around at the other raccoons, who seemed to be building blanket forts with some bedding they'd found. He took a deep breath and let it out slowly. (Butterbean had the distinct impression he was also counting to ten.)

"I see your point," Oscar said, frowning. It was true, those didn't look like raccoons who would do well in captivity. And that was the best-case scenario.

Oscar clicked his beak in frustration. If the raccoons got caught in the act, it would definitely clear Madison's name. But Reginald was right. He hadn't fully appreciated the risk to the raccoons.

Oscar stepped forward and gave a slight bow. "Reginald, I have to apologize. I wasn't considering the implications." He turned to the others. "We'll have to come up with something else."

"But what other options do we have? There's nothing else. What are we supposed to do?" Walt demanded. "Frame someone? Because I can't think—"

"Well, look at that." The white cat stalked into the storage area flanked by Marco, Polo, and Wallace. She sat down and shot an accusing look at Walt and the others. "I thought we'd be leading a rescue expedition, but it looks like somebody forgot to invite us to a party."

Walt and Oscar exchanged a significant glance.

"You left us behind!" Polo complained, stomping up to Butterbean.

"You should've told us," Marco muttered.

"Yeah," Wallace said weakly. He still hadn't quite woken up.

"And you're buddy-buddy with this guy now?" The white cat nodded toward the big raccoon. "Weren't you saying something about threats, Oscar?"

A raccoon wearing a tutu reached out slowly toward the button around Polo's neck. Polo shot him a nervous side eye and edged closer to the white cat.

Oscar shifted his weight awkwardly. "Well, see, Butterbean did some therapy . . ."

"Oh, of course. Butterbean did therapy. It's all clear now." The white cat rolled her eyes as she smacked the tutu raccoon's hand away. "Puh-leaze."

"It's true!" Butterbean said. "And the raccoons are going to help us clear Madison."

"Oh, so they're confessing to Bob? Is that it?" The white cat twitched her tail. "Again, I say, PUH-LEAZE."

Walt shot another significant look to Oscar.

"So we were just um, thinking about you, actually," Walt said to the white cat in her sweetest voice. "About what a talented actor you are." She nudged Oscar hard.

Oscar snapped to attention. "Right. So talented." He swallowed nervously. "And we were hoping . . . well, we were thinking we could um, hire you? Maybe?"

Butterbean's eyes grew wide. "OOH! RIGHT! I get it! Like last time! That would be perfect!"

The white cat had done them a favor once, giving a showstopping performance to help get the animals out of some trouble. (She'd done an amazing job. Residents of the building were still talking about it. At least, the white cat was still talking about it.)

The white cat inspected her paw. "So let me get this straight. You're thinking that I'll step in and save the day for you again by pretending *I'm* the one who made this mess? Is that it?"

"Yes?" Butterbean said hopefully.

"No," the white cat sniffed. "I have an exclusive contract with Beautiful Buffet Cat Food, remember?"

She waved the package of caviar treats in the air. "I couldn't help even if I wanted to. No more side gigs. Sorry."

"I'm sorry, who is this?" Reginald said, staring at the white cat with a baffled expression.

"Um, excuse me. Could I . . ." Two small, thin hands were trying to grab at the waving treat package. The white cat looked down to see the small raccoon wearing a tube top wiggling its fingers in anticipation. "Would you mind if . . ." the raccoon said in a tiny voice.

The white cat tossed the package to the raccoon. "Oh, please, take the whole thing. You're doing me a favor."

The small raccoon took a treat, examined it, and hurried over to the utility sink to wash it carefully. Then she took a delicate bite. "Oh yes, thank you. Very nice," she said, her eyes shining. She took one more and then tucked the package into her tube top.

The white cat's eyebrows shot up. "At least somebody likes them," she muttered.

"LISTEN UP!" Reginald clapped his hands loudly. "Here's the solution. We'll just stop, okay?" He scratched his stomach. "This place is getting old anyway, what with that lady and that maintenance guy always snooping around. Besides, we've already found most of the good stuff."

Butterbean looked at Walt and Oscar. "That sounds good, right? If they just stop? It'll be all solved then!"

"Well . . ." A strange look crossed Oscar's face.

Reginald nodded. "Done." He turned to the raccoons behind him. "NEW RULE! No more messing things up, okay? From now on everything goes back where you found it."

"Oooohhhhh." The raccoons gave a half-hearted thumbs-up before continuing on with what looked like a costume party. (Except for the group in the corner, which had started what sounded like a barbershop quartet.)

"NO!" Oscar said suddenly. "No no no, that's the absolute worst thing you could do. Do NOT stop."

"But that's what we want, isn't it? For them to stop?" Butterbean was so confused. It was late, and she'd put in a long night of work already. Being a therapist was harder than she'd thought.

"Don't you see? If they stop now, it'll look like it was Madison all along," Oscar said. "Think about it. She's not coming down here anymore. So if it stops . . ."

"They'll still think it was her!" Butterbean said. "We need to make it worse, right?"

Reginald sighed and clapped his hands again. "LISTEN UP! Change of plans. DO NOT put things back where you found them. Let's mess this place up!"

"WHOOHOO!" The raccoons gave a much more enthusiastic thumbs-up and cheer and flung various bits of clothing into the air. Chad even clapped from the sink (splashing the harmonica raccoon in the process).

"Thank you," Oscar said to Reginald after the cheering had ended. "I think this will work."

"It has to," Butterbean said.

"We'll make sure it does," Reginald said. He nudged Butterbean. "And don't worry, Doc. We'll put that lady's stuff back where she's sure to see it. Clear the kid's name."

"Thanks," Butterbean said, beaming. "You're a very good patient."

Reginald's ears turned pink. "Well, you know. Felt good to talk to someone."

"Doc?" Walt stared at Butterbean for a long second and then shook her head.

Reginald picked up a throw pillow and tore it in half with his bare hands. "Now, you guys clear out. We've got a mess to make!" he said, throwing the fluff in the air.

"Um. Yes. Thanks again," Oscar said, edging carefully out of the room.

As they waited for the elevator, Oscar felt hopeful for the first time in a long time. "You did it, Butterbean," he said quietly as he took his place on her head. "You fixed it. Trust me, by tomorrow morning, everything will be back to normal."

– 16 –

Everything was not back to normal. It was worse.

They'd expected to get good news about Madison first thing in the morning, but as the day stretched on, the animals started to get concerned. So when the knock on the door finally came, Butterbean leaped to her feet in excitement. "Finally! Madison's been cleared!"

"Shh, Butterbean, be calm," Mrs. Food said, wiping her hands on a dish towel as she walked to the door.

"Sheesh, it took long enough," Marco grumbled, hopping onto the water bottle for a better view.

"Too bad Madison's at school," Polo said. "She's going to miss the whole thing!"

"It's probably Bob coming to apologize," Oscar said smugly. "This will be good."

The animals watched in anticipation as Mrs. Food opened the door. They were half-right—it was Bob. But he wasn't coming to apologize. In fact, he'd barely opened his mouth to speak when he was pushed aside by Mrs. Hates Dogs on Six.

"Well, I was right," Mrs. Hates Dogs on Six gloated. "What do you have to say for yourself?"

"Sorry to disturb you, Mrs. Fudeker." Bob made an apologetic face over Mrs. Hates Dogs on Six's head. "But there's been a new development."

"I have PROOF," Mrs. Hates Dogs on Six said, waving a handful of papers in Mrs. Food's face. "PROOF right here. I knew it was that girl—I just knew it!"

Mrs. Food frowned and pushed the papers aside. "What proof could you possibly have? Madison didn't do anything wrong."

"That little vandal did it AGAIN, and I can PROVE IT." Mrs. Hates Dogs on Six had a nasty gleam in her eye.

Walt and Oscar exchanged a concerned look. This wasn't how things were supposed to go.

"The storage area was vandalized again last night, Mrs. Fudeker, and it was worse than before," Bob said. "And it looks like . . ." He glanced at Mrs. Hates Dogs on Six. "Well, it was strange. There were some things that are hard to explain."

"Look here, see? PHOTOGRAPHIC EVIDENCE." Mrs. Hates Dogs on Six pushed the papers at Mrs. Food again. "Bob took these this morning. See right here?" She jabbed her finger at one of the pictures.

Mrs. Food took the pictures and examined them closely. Then she looked up with a confused expression on her face. "What am I looking at here? Madison isn't in this picture," Mrs. Food said. "I'm sorry about the damage—it does look bad. But I don't see how this involves us at all."

"Oh you don't, do you?" Mrs. Hates Dogs on Six pointed harder at the picture. "See that? That's my stolen property. All lined up in a row. And look at THAT." She pointed again.

Mrs. Food looked at the picture again, more closely this time. Then she turned pale. "Well." She looked up at Bob, who made another apologetic face. "Well, that is odd. I admit that. But I can't explain it. Madison and I were both here all last night. We didn't even go down to the storage area."

"I haven't figured out how she did it, but trust me, you're going to be prosecuted for this," Mrs. Hates Dogs on Six smirked. "I'll see to it."

Mrs. Food tried to give the pictures back, but Mrs.

Hates Dogs on Six pushed her hands away. "Oh, you keep those, Beulah. You'll need them for your lawyers. And believe me, I had extra copies made. So many copies."

"Okay, you've had your say." Bob gently pulled Mrs. Hates Dogs on Six back from the door. "Now I'll handle this from here, okay?"

Mrs. Hates Dogs on Six opened her mouth to protest, but Bob held up his hand. "It all needs to be official, understand?" he said. "I can't have Mrs. Fudeker here making a harassment complaint against you."

Mrs. Hates Dogs on Six snapped her mouth shut, whirled around, and huffed away.

Bob waited until she'd gone before he turned back to Mrs. Food.

"That harassment complaint, that's something you have legitimate grounds for, you know." He ran his hand over his head. "Now, you'll swear that you and Madison weren't anywhere near that storage unit?"

"We didn't leave the apartment," Mrs. Food said.

"And Madison will swear to that too?"

Mrs. Food nodded.

"Okay, okay," Bob said thoughtfully. "Because those pictures, they don't look good. I don't know how to explain those."

"I know."

Bob sighed and rubbed his face. "I'll try and sort

this out. But I'll probably need you to come down and make an official statement for the board," he said.

"Thank you, Bob," Mrs. Food said calmly. But she was clutching the photos a little too tightly.

She closed the door quietly, and in one quick motion, she threw the photos onto the table. Then she stormed off down the hall.

"She's mad," Butterbean said softly as she watched Mrs. Food disappear into her office.

"The photos, Walt," Oscar said. "Quick. What's in the photos?"

Walt jumped up onto the table and pawed through them, examining them carefully. Then she looked up, her face stormy. "Those raccoons have messed up everything."

There was no getting around it—they had to talk to Reginald.

It didn't matter that it was the middle of the day. They had to risk it. Operation Cleanup was too important. (That was what they'd decided to call it. Butterbean voted for Operation Get the Raccoons to Explain What the Heck Went Wrong So They Could Help Restore Madison's Reputation, but everyone agreed that spy missions needed to have slightly shorter names.)

Dunkin knew where the tube-top raccoon usually slept, and the white cat was sent on her first secret spy mission. Luckily it was a success. With the help of a few caviar treats, she was able to convince the tube-top raccoon to take her to Reginald, who she persuaded to come for a secret spy meeting in Mrs. Food's apartment. (He was less than happy about the whole situation. Apparently some of the vents had been a pretty tight squeeze.)

He didn't get any happier once they confronted him with the photos.

"I'm sorry, but we did what we said. I don't see how any of this is our fault!" Reginald said, his hands on his hips. "And I'm not too pleased to have your flunkies SUMMONING ME."

"Excuse me?" the white cat scowled. "Mysterious Spy on a Mission of Mercy, IF YOU PLEASE."

"It was urgent," Walt explained. "We had no choice!"

"I tried to tell him," the white cat said, sitting down. "And I'm hardly a FLUNKIE."

Oscar cleared his throat and dropped the most incriminating photo down on the floor. "Reginald, I apologize for bringing you here. But take a look again. I'm sure you'll see this called for drastic measures."

Reginald picked up the photo and looked at it briefly. "What? We trashed the place, just like we said we would."

"Not exactly like you said," Polo piped up.

"EXACTLY like we said." Reginald glared at the rats.

"Except?" Oscar prodded.

"Except?" Reginald looked confused. "Except what? Oh! Except for yours. We figured you wouldn't want us trashing your stuff, right, guys?" Reginald called over his shoulder at the couch. "Wasn't that nice of us?"

The tube-top raccoon peeked her head out from behind the couch. She was quickly joined by more raccoons, each peeking their heads out until the whole side of the couch was nothing but raccoon faces.

"Oh, that's not good," Walt said, shooting a look at the apartment door. Mrs. Food had gone downstairs to meet with Bob, but they had no idea how long that meeting was going to take.

"Who are these guys?" Butterbean gasped. "Tulip, is that you?"

"You KNOW her?" Marco said, staring at Butterbean. He had a feeling he'd missed a lot while he was asleep.

The tube-top raccoon waved shyly. "Hi, Butterbean." She nudged one of the other raccoons. "She knows my NAME!" she whispered excitedly.

"You brought an ENTOURAGE?" Walt asked, turning on Reginald.

"Look, where I go, they go. It's how we operate."

Reginald looked at the photo again. "So what's your problem, exactly?"

"Look at that photo. Can't you see how suspicious it all looks?" Walt said, lashing her tail in frustration. "The whole room is trashed except for ONE UNIT. And that's the unit belonging to Mrs. Food and Madison."

"Yeah, but who's going to notice that," Reginald scoffed. "We did you a favor."

"MRS. HATES DOGS ON SIX NOTICED!" Butterbean barked. "She came over and was MEAN."

"Oh, that lady," Reginald rolled her eyes. "You know, she should've just been happy to get her stuff back. We made sure we put it out in a safe place. Right where it was easy to see."

"Yes, about that," Oscar said, controlling his voice carefully. "You put it out IN MRS. FOOD AND MADISON'S STORAGE UNIT."

"WHICH WAS LOCKED," Walt added.

"Well, yeah. Since that one wasn't trashed, it would be easy to spot." Reginald said. "Duh." The other raccoons murmured in agreement. One of them plucked a few notes on what sounded like a ukulele.

Oscar shut his eyes. "You trashed the entire room. Except for the unit that belongs to Madison. You put the stolen merchandise in Madison's unit. Which was locked. And one of the only people to have a key was Madison. And this is supposed to clear Madison's name?"

It was like a light bulb went off over Reginald's head. He made a face. "Oh. Yeah, that. Hmm. Yeah, that does seem kind of bad," he admitted. "Okay, I see it now. So, what, should we trash your unit too? Because we can do that."

The raccoons nodded and looked hopeful.

"Oh, Bob will LOVE that," the white cat said sarcastically.

Oscar shook his head. "I don't think that will work. Mrs. Hates Dogs on Six will just think Madison managed to sneak in somehow. That's what she already thinks."

"And Madison can't even fit in the vents!" Butterbean said.

"We've got to come up with something else. Something big," Walt said. A harmonica started playing somewhere in the corner of the room. "If we all work together, we can figure this out. I know we can." The harmonica accompaniment continued as she spoke, this time punctuated by random notes from a musical triangle. It sounded like she was doing a dramatic speech from a movie.

"Madison is depending on us. We can't let her

down. We can't just— Excuse me, do you mind?" Walt whipped her head around to look at the tall raccoon in the corner. He lowered the harmonica and blushed.

"Sorry about that," the raccoon said, tucking the harmonica behind his back. He bowed his head in apology.

Ding! The stocky raccoon with the triangle accented the move.

Walt whipped her head around again. "You too, buddy."

The raccoon clutched the vibrating triangle to his chest.

"Where'd you get that, anyway?" Butterbean asked, going over and examining the triangle. "Was that in the storage area?" She hadn't realized raccoons were so musical. She sniffed at the triangle. It smelled like it belonged to Old Mothball Lady on two. Butterbean shrank back. She hated mothballs.

The stocky raccoon clung to the triangle protectively. "Reginald said we didn't have to put things back, so it's okay that I took it. Right?" He looked to Reginald for confirmation.

"Right." Reginald nodded.

"So how many of you raccoons have instruments, anyway?" The white cat stood up and stalked around the room. "Is it just you two?"

The raccoons exchanged awkward looks, shrinking back as the white cat approached.

"Come on, don't be shy. We've got a triangle and a harmonica. Anyone else?" The white cat stopped short in front of two fluffy raccoons hiding something behind their backs.

"Come on. Give. What is it?" The white cat loomed over them, somehow making herself look huge and fierce.

The raccoons held out a ukulele almost as big as they were.

The white cat nodded and then stalked back to Oscar. She sat down with a smirk on her face.

"Problem solved," she said. "I know what we're going to do."

– 17 –

"YOU CALL THOSE HIGH KICKS? GET THOSE legs up!" The white cat clapped her paws as she circled around a line of raccoons attempting to dance the can can. She turned to Oscar. "I always wanted to direct."

Oscar couldn't believe they'd actually agreed to the white cat's plan. It was definitely risky. But it was the only plan they had.

Once they'd worked out everyone's role in Operation Dazzle (which is what the white cat had named it), there had been one big problem left—finding a place for the rehearsal. Luckily the raccoons knew the perfect spot.

"I can't believe we're practicing in the STORAGE

AREA," Walt said, flattening her ears down and shooting a nervous look at the basement door.

"REHEARSING." The white cat sounded disgusted. "We're REHEARSING in the PERFORMANCE SPACE. And it's FINE." She clapped in time to the raccoons' high kicks.

Since Mrs. Hates Dogs on Six had started threatening lawsuits, Bob had cordoned off the entire room. And according to the rats, that meant that it was the only place they were guaranteed not to be interrupted. The raccoons agreed.

The white cat had wasted no time setting up the performance space, as she called it, and getting to work. (She said "storage area" sounded unprofessional.)

"Are you sure this is the way we should do this?" Oscar asked, hopping to keep up with her. "I thought we were just going to adjust the surveillance camera so they would see the raccoons."

The white cat stopped in her tracks. "Well, sure, but why go small when we could go BIG!" She pulled Oscar slightly to the side. "Besides, based on the screen test we did, you need my talents," she whispered.

"We did a screen test?" Oscar looked at Walt. "When did we do a screen test?"

"That's what she's calling 'checking the surveillance

camera,'" Walt said, rolling her eyes. "I thought we could just catch the raccoons onscreen. But Madam Director here didn't think it was good enough."

"Do you want a couple of blurry raccoon-shaped blobs on film, or do you want SPECTACLE?" the white cat said. "Trust me, with my skills, these guys are going to POP." The white cat made explosion motions with her paws. "These raccoons may not have the most talent, but with my vision, this is going to be HUGE."

"Do we want huge, though?" Walt said in a low voice. "I thought we just wanted to clear Madison's name."

"Why can't we do both?" the white cat said distractedly as she waved at a group of raccoons awkwardly holding instruments. "Let's try it with the music now." She clapped again.

Wallace and Dunkin slipped into the room from one of the vents. "We've got the rat costumes. Where do you want them?" Dunkin had his arms filled with tiny clothes, and Wallace held out the little sailor shirt he'd been wearing before. He shot an apologetic look at Oscar. "We're just borrowing them. It's for a good cause. We'll put them back, I promise."

"Rat costumes?" Oscar said slowly. "That seems—"

The white cat put a paw up to his beak. "Look, you

have your role, I have mine. Just let me do my job. I've been in this business for a while, don't forget."

Oscar and Walt exchanged a long look.

The white cat leaned in again. "And I'm thinking the rats will be background performers. FAR in the background."

"I suppose that's . . . fine?" Oscar said (although his voice was muffled by the furry paw.)

"Sure. Why not," Walt said with a shrug. She wasn't about to argue with that cat. As long as Madison's reputation was restored and everything got back to normal, it probably didn't matter how they got there.

At least she hoped so.

"So it's all set up?" Polo asked. "We used the remote to change the channel on the Television. It was tougher than it looks!"

"It's okay, though. I've been working out," Marco said, flexing his arm muscles. (Not too much, though— they were a little sore.)

Marco and Polo had campaigned to be part of the basement stage crew, but Oscar had thought it would be better for them to stick closer to home, in case they needed to run any messages downstairs. Because there wasn't much time. Once Madison got home, they'd activate Operation Dazzle.

Oscar couldn't believe everything was riding on an operation with such a ridiculous name. And on the white cat.

"Good job, you two. The raccoons are rehearsing downstairs," Oscar said. "I hope that cat knows what she's doing."

"If you need any distractions, just let me know," Butterbean said from her position by the door. "I'm happy to distract."

"Thank you, Butterbean," Oscar said. "I think we're set. We'll just wait for Madison now." The animals all turned to look at the door.

"I've got ideas," Butterbean said after a few minutes of silence. She'd been working on some new techniques that she was itching to try out. She especially wanted to try out her new move of "accidentally" locking herself in the bathroom. She thought that would be particularly distracting.

"Is this the bathroom thing?" Oscar said. (Butterbean talked in her sleep sometimes.)

"Yep!" Butterbean nodded. "How did you know?"

"I think we should keep that as a last resort," Oscar said. He had a feeling that might be too big a distraction.

Walt looked from Butterbean to Oscar and then back again.

"What's the bathroom thing?" Walt said finally. Then she made a face. "Actually? Never mind. I don't need to know."

Oscar nodded. "Wise choice." He cleared his throat. "Now, while we wait . . . does everyone know what to do?"

"Yep," Butterbean said, thumping her tail. "Take Madison for a walk, and then I start the show!"

"Right." Oscar hoped Butterbean was clear on what "starting the show" was supposed to mean, but he had to have faith. He was ready to improvise if there were any problems. "Marco? Polo?"

"Emergency runners," Polo said. "In case of disaster."

"You can count on us," Marco said, doing some stretches. "Like I said, I've been—"

"Working out. Yes, that's great," Oscar said.

"We could go down now if you want, though," Polo said. "Just saying. Or if you need more performers . . ." She trailed off hopefully.

"Noted." Oscar turned to Walt. "Walt?"

Walt shot him a disgusted glance. "Do you have to ask?"

"No. Of course, you know what to do," Oscar said. "I just wanted to make sure that—"

The door opened, and Madison hurried inside. "I'm home!" she called, dumping her book bag on the floor. "Any news?"

"SHE'S HERE!" Butterbean screamed, jumping up. (And promptly falling over again. She'd been sitting for so long her feet had fallen asleep.)

"Oh no, are you okay?" Madison bent down to rub Butterbean's ears. (That was another reason Butterbean had positioned herself by the door. Better chance of ear rubs.)

Mrs. Food hurried in from her office. "Madison, you're home!"

Madison looked up. "So have I been exonerated yet?"

Mrs. Food answered with a weak smile. "Not exactly. But I'm working on the situation. You'll see."

"I know," Madison said gloomily. "I just hate this."

"I know," Mrs. Food said, patting her on the shoulder.

Oscar hopped from his perch to the side of his cage. "Walt! Mrs. Food's out of the office! You're up."

Walt nodded discreetly and disappeared down the hall into the office.

Butterbean looked up at Oscar. "Operation Dazzle?" Oscar nodded. "Starts now."

⪦⪡⪢⪡⪢⪡⪢⪡⪢⪡⪢⪡⪢

Butterbean thought she must've set a record for taking the fastest walk in the history of dog walks. She practically dragged Madison inside after she'd finished doing her business. She was very proud of herself. She hadn't stopped to smell a single bush.

Madison unclipped the leash as they came inside, shaking her head. "I don't know what's wrong with her. It's like she was running a race."

"Good job, Bean," Oscar said approvingly. So far the plan was going smoothly.

"Are we all set?" Butterbean asked as she trotted inside. "I'm ready for my big part."

Walt stalked down the hallway and sat down, licking her paw. "Done."

Oscar fluffed his feathers anxiously. "Good, good." Walt had some impressive computer skills. "So that means things should start happening . . ."

"Any minute now," Walt said. "Marco? Wheels are in motion. Let them know."

Marco leaped onto the water bottle. "WHOOO-HOOO, emergency run!"

"No need. We're ready too." The white cat popped her head out from behind the couch.

"What?" Marco dropped back down to the floor. "No emergency run?"

Polo gasped. "But you're supposed to be in the storage area!"

The white cat rolled her eyes. "I will be. I'm just waiting for the fireworks. Once those start, I'll head down and start the show."

Oscar's eyes widened in horror. "Fireworks? No one said anything about fireworks." He whipped around to look at Walt. "Did you know she was getting FIREWORKS?"

The doorbell rang. The white cat rolled her eyes. "No, silly, not that kind of fireworks." She nodded toward the door. "These fireworks."

"I wonder who . . ." Mrs. Food muttered to herself.

She opened the door. It was Mrs. Hates Dogs on Six.

"Oh. I see. That kind of fireworks," Oscar said in relief. Although from what he could tell, it was more like an ice storm than fireworks.

The white cat cackled loudly. "We'll be ready in five." She disappeared again behind the couch.

"Here we go," Walt said, watching the scene at the door. "I just hope it works."

"Harriet." Mrs. Food's voice was frosty. "To what do I owe this pleasure?"

"Very funny," Mrs. Hates Dogs on Six said. "As if you don't know."

"Who's at the . . ." Madison came into the living room. "Oh."

Mrs. Hates Dogs on Six sniffed. "Oh, is she still here?"

"Um. Hi." Madison turned bright red. She gave a short, awkward wave.

"Where are the fireworks?" Butterbean whispered to Walt. She hadn't realized they were part of the plan.

"Forget the fireworks," Walt hissed. "I'll explain later."

Mrs. Food gave a sharp laugh. "Of course Madison's still here," Mrs. Food said. "Now if you don't mind—"

There was a ding from the hallway, and Bob jogged up behind Mrs. Hates Dogs on Six. "Oh, hi, good, you're both here. Hope I'm not too late."

Mrs. Food frowned. "Too late for what?"

"The meeting?" Bob frowned back. "Our little chat?" He turned to Mrs. Food. "To be honest, I was relieved when I got your call. I think getting together and clearing the air is a great idea. Hopefully we can straighten this all out."

"My call? But . . ." Mrs. Food stared at him

open-mouthed for a long second, before turning to look at Madison. Madison shrugged.

Walt licked her paw smugly.

"Well, I'm not meeting in the hallway," Mrs. Hates Dogs on Six said snippily.

"No, of course not. Come in." Mrs. Food stood back. "For our meeting." She sounded like she'd gritted her teeth on that last word.

Mrs. Hates Dogs on Six walked into the room, clasping her hands in front of her chest like she was afraid to touch anything.

"Please, have a seat," Mrs. Food said.

Mrs. Hates Dogs on Six looked down at the couch like it was something Walt had just coughed up. She sat down gingerly, perching on the extreme edge of the cushion.

Mrs. Food sat in the chair closest to her, and Madison half sat on the arm.

"So, now, I'd like to start, if I could," Bob said, sitting down and leaning forward on his knees like he was some kind of coach. "Now, first off, I want to say that we have no direct evidence implicating Madison in this crime."

"Thank you," Madison said.

"But we don't have any evidence implicating anyone else, either. And we don't have any evidence that it WASN'T Madison."

"But I told you—" Madison started.

"I'm sorry, but I've heard enough," Mrs. Food said, standing up. "Madison's word is good enough for me. I think this meeting is over."

"Mrs. Fudeker, please—"

"Butterbean! You're on!" Oscar squawked. Things were moving faster than they'd expected.

Everything depended on Butterbean. Everything.

Taking huge strides, Butterbean raced across the floor and lunged up at the coffee table.

"Control your ANIMAL!" Mrs. Hates Dogs on Six screeched, reeling back in her seat.

Butterbean ignored her. She knew what she had to do. With one last lunge, Butterbean slammed her foot onto the Television remote.

And the Television came on.

— 18 —

AND IMMEDIATELY CHANGED TO THE HOME Shopping Channel.

"Butterbean, no!" Mrs. Food leaned forward to grab her. "I apologize for my dog."

Mrs. Hates Dogs on Six had shrunk back so far against the couch cushions that it looked like she was going to climb on top of them.

"I'll get her," Madison said, getting up to come around the coffee table.

"That's the wrong channel!" Oscar screeched. "Hit the down button! Or the up button! Change it back to the surveillance camera!"

Butterbean hit the remote again. It changed to the Hallmark Channel.

"NOOOO!" Butterbean wailed as she smacked the channel changer again. A show with a car chase came on. "I'm sorry!" She smacked at it again. The volume went up. "I should've practiced!"

"Control that dog!" Mrs. Hates Dogs on Six said, raising her feet off the floor, like she thought Butterbean was going to go for her toes.

"I've got her," Madison said, scrambling to pick Butterbean up. "She's not usually like this. She's going to be a therapy dog."

"That dog? I doubt it," Mrs. Hates Dogs on Six sniffed.

"I am SO!" Butterbean lunged so she was half dangling from Madison's arms and flailed her front paws, smacking at the remote repeatedly. The channel flicked back and forth quickly, and finally landed on a black-and-white-camera shot. The surveillance camera in the basement.

"That's the one! Stop!" Walt yowled. "STOP!"

"I'm sorry, Oscar!" Butterbean moaned as Madison carried her into the kitchen.

Oscar didn't answer. His focus was on the camera footage of the storage area. The *empty* storage area. He looked at Walt, his eyes wide.

There were no raccoons anywhere.

The white cat hurried down the row of raccoons, fluffing whiskers and smoothing down wispy tufts of hair. Then she clapped her paws.

"Okay, you know what to do! Raccoons, center stage. Band, stage right. Singers, stage left. We're going to knock their socks off!"

Wallace nudged her and pointed to a group of rats standing awkwardly to the side. "Where should the rats go?" They were dressed in sailor suits, pinafores, and tiny nightgowns. One of them was wearing a bonnet.

The white cat hesitated and then waved her paw vaguely in the direction of the stage. "Rats, um, upstage."

She turned to Reginald, who was standing to the side, wearing an oversized, fringy leather vest and a cowboy hat. "Are you ready?"

"Let's do this," Reginald said, adjusting his hat.

The white cat looked up at Chad, who was hanging from the surveillance camera. He looked like he was asleep. "Chad! Curtain up!"

Chad opened one eye and adjusted the surveillance camera. "Voilà. Curtain up."

The white cat clapped her paws. "Places, everyone! You're on!"

Walt glanced at Oscar uneasily and then turned back to the empty storage area onscreen. "Where are they? That's the right channel."

"I don't know," Oscar said. Butterbean had hit the wrong button at first, but they'd fixed it. It had only been a few minutes. Surely they hadn't missed it?

Mrs. Food picked up the Television remote. "I apologize again. I'll just turn this off."

"NOOOOO!" Walt's voice was a low growl.

Mrs. Food pointed the remote at the Television. Then she hesitated.

Something had appeared on the screen.

Mrs. Food's jaw dropped.

Everyone in the room stared in silence for a few long minutes. Then Mrs. Food leaned forward. "Is that?" She got up and took a few steps closer. "I'm sorry, is that . . ."

Oscar held his breath.

"WHAT ARE THOSE?" Mrs. Hates Dogs on Six shrieked. "Are those BEARS?"

"BEARS?" Butterbean barked from the kitchen. "Where?"

Mrs. Food put down the remote and squinted at the television. "No, I think they're . . ."

"BEARS OR DOGS. That's disgusting!" Mrs.

Hates Dogs on Six turned on Bob. "There are BEARS in the storage area!"

Madison hurried back in, bouncing Butterbean up and down like a baby. "What's going on? What bears?"

Mrs. Food walked closer to the Television and peered at the screen closely. "I think those are . . . I'm not sure . . ."

"RACCOONS," Bob growled, staring at the screen. "Those are RACCOONS." Bob sounded like raccoons were his mortal enemy.

"But are those COSTUMES?" Mrs. Food frowned in disbelief.

"Don't be ridiculous," Mrs. Hates Dogs on Six sputtered. "Those are . . . Bob, what are those?"

"Walt, can you turn up the sound?" Oscar said in a low voice. "I can't hear anything."

Walt nodded and slunk over to the coffee table on her stomach.

Onscreen, the raccoons were doing an admirable cancan, with lots of high kicks and jazz hands. The white cat had done something with the lighting in the storage area, and although Oscar almost hated to admit it, she'd been right. Those raccoons really popped onscreen.

Suddenly Reginald, wearing his cowboy outfit, leaped into the center of the stage, mugging for the

camera as he sang an obviously heartfelt rendition of . . .
something. The problem was that there was no sound.

Mrs. Hates Dogs on Six gasped. "THAT BEAR
IS WEARING MY HAT!" she shrieked, pointing at
the screen.

Walt pounced on the remote and hit the volume
button. But nothing happened. She turned to Oscar,
her eyes wide. "There's no sound. THIS CHANNEL
HAS NO SOUND!"

They turned back and stared at the silent television in dismay.

All that rehearsal had been for nothing.

"Reginald, catch!" The white cat tossed a ukulele to Reginald, who caught it and immediately started a heartbreaking rendition of a traditional raccoon cowboy song. The white cat nudged Wallace, who was watching with tears in his eyes. (He'd always been a sucker for sad songs.) "Here, take this." She handed him a small camera phone.

"What's this?" Wallace said, struggling to hold it up. It was about the same size he was.

"Don't ask questions—just push that button when I tell you," the white cat said. "You're a cameraman now."

"Okay?" Wallace said. It was always good to add new skills to his résumé.

The white cat waved to the tube-top raccoon standing on the sidelines. "You! Sparkles!"

The tube-top raccoon looked around and then pointed at herself questioningly. "I'm Tulip?"

"Tulip, get out there! Show them what you've got," the white cat said. "Do that move you were doing earlier. I've got a surprise for you."

Tulip's face lit up and she raced out in front of the camera.

It was her big shot.

"Are those maracas?" Madison asked, peering at the screen.

"Those are RACCOONS," Bob said, his face turning deeper and deeper red. "In MY STORAGE AREA."

"No, I meant the . . . never mind," Madison said. She knew the difference between raccoons and maracas. Madison looked around for the remote. "Does this channel have sound?"

"NO!" Oscar and Walt wailed.

"Guys, I don't think it matters. I think it's working!" Butterbean said, craning her neck to get a better view of the screen. It was hard to see, because Madison's big head was blocking her view.

"Why is that little one so sparkly?" Mrs. Food asked, squinting. "I swear, it looks like it's wearing an outfit." Onscreen, Tulip's sequined tube top caught the light as she did her best interpretive dance, complete with elaborate arm waving.

"Excuse me," Bob said, pushing his chair back and rushing to the door. "I have to . . . RACCOONS," he bellowed as he ran out into the hallway.

"Marco! You're on!" Oscar called, jumping onto the side of his cage. "We have to warn them!"

Marco was way ahead of him. He'd already crawled out of the cage and was racing across the floor toward the vent.

"Wait for me!" Polo said, disappearing behind the couch after him.

"Sparkles! Catch!" The white cat tossed something to Tulip, who caught it awkwardly against her chest. "Hit record, Wallace. NOW!"

Wallace hit record.

Tulip looked down at what was in her hands. It was the packet of cat treats.

"Hold it up for the camera!" the white cat said. "That's right, so we get a clear shot. Now eat!"

Tulip froze. "But . . . I need to wash . . ."

"I washed it for you already," the white cat said. "Dig in! Reginald, you too. Take a treat as a reward for a job well done. And really SELL IT!" The raccoons clustered around Tulip as she handed out the treats. Then they ate them with much lip smacking and tummy rubbing. (They were a little over the top, actually.)

"Perfect!" The white cat cheered.

Wallace folded his arms and looked at the white cat disapprovingly.

"What? White lie. They're clean!" The white cat shrugged.

"He's coming!" Marco's screech filled the room as he did a sliding run into the basement from the vent.

"RUN, YOU GUYS!" Polo yelled. They'd slipped down the vents like they were on a water slide, so they'd made it in record time. Polo looked at the door nervously. The apartment elevators were slow, but not that slow. "Bob's on his way!"

They didn't have much time.

The white cat nodded calmly. "Take your bows, everyone. And GO!"

The raccoons did elaborate hammy bows, grabbed their instruments and props, and then scattered, squeezing into the vents and slipping out through the holes in the insulation with one last wave goodbye.

"What was that? What were they EATING?" Mrs. Food asked. She and Mrs. Hates Dogs on Six were both kneeling in front of the Television to get the best possible view.

"Where are they going? Are they leaving? That one still has my hat!" Mrs. Hates Dogs on Six said. "And where is Bob?"

"There!" Madison stopped bouncing Butterbean up and down and pointed at the screen. "He's coming in now."

Onscreen, they could see Bob storm into the storage area and look around wildly, picking up bits of clothing and boxes as he searched for the raccoons. Then he turned in a slow circle, hands on hips as he scanned the room.

But there was nothing. The raccoons were gone.

Walt looked up at Oscar and gave an approving nod.

Operation Dazzle was a success.

— 19 —

"So, yeah. Raccoons," Bob said when he came back upstairs. "I didn't catch them, but that's definitely what they were. It looks like they got into pretty much everything."

"So. Raccoons." Mrs. Food turned to look at Mrs. Hates Dogs on Six. "Did you hear that, Harriet? Raccoons were in the storage area."

Mrs. Hates Dogs on Six shifted uncomfortably and smoothed her skirt. "Well, what do you know." She looked up at Bob. "So they were responsible for the damage?"

"Yup," Bob said.

"This whole time?"

"Looks like it." Bob crossed his arms.

"Hmm. Well, well." Mrs. Hates Dogs on Six looked at Madison and took a deep breath. "Then I apologize."

Madison's eyebrows shot up. "Wow. Okay, um. Thanks."

Mrs. Hates Dogs on Six sniffed. "I said it, no need to go on about it. Gloating is never attractive." She looked down at Butterbean. "And control your dog. I don't want to have to tell you again."

She nodded briefly at Bob and Mrs. Food and then marched to the door, her back stiff.

"Well, I guess that's the best you're going to get," Bob said after the door had shut behind her.

"I think we'll take that as a win," Mrs. Food said, patting Madison on the back.

"Good. And for the record, I'm sorry too." Bob rubbed his hand over his face. "I wasn't going to let her have you arrested."

"Wait, WHAT?" Madison's jaw dropped as she looked from Bob to Mrs. Food. "She wanted to have me ARRESTED?"

"Sooo," Bob said, a panicked expression on his face. "If you'll excuse me, I have some raccoons to deal with." He turned and bolted for the door.

Madison turned to Mrs. Food, her arms crossed. "ARRESTED?"

"You mean you couldn't hear ANY of it?" The white cat's face fell. "But the music really made the production. They were terrific. Reginald's song . . ." The white cat put her paw over her heart. "It got you right here."

After Bob had left, Mrs. Food had taken Madison out for ice cream to celebrate her vindication (and to help her get over the whole "arrested" thing). Which meant that Mrs. Food's apartment was the perfect location for the white cat's cast party. Oscar tried to protest (no one had told him about a cast party), but it's hard to say no when hordes of happy raccoons and rats are streaming into your apartment.

"It looked amazing, even without sound. It did the trick. It doesn't matter that we couldn't hear it," Oscar said, watching carefully to make sure no one knocked anything over.

"But the harmonies! And that ukulele solo!" The white cat shook her head despairingly. "Well, that's it. We'll have to do it again."

"We're not doing it again," Reginald said, laughing and clapping the white cat on the back. "But I have to admit, that was fun. Maybe I should've had a singing career."

"Oh, you still could," the white cat said with a gleam in her eye. "Wallace, do you have that phone?"

Wallace nodded, dragging the camera phone behind him. He dropped it at the white cat's feet and then leaned over with his hands on his knees, breathing heavily. "I don't want to be a cameraman anymore."

"That's fine," the white cat said, swiping at the screen. "You can add social media manager to your résumé too. Because that video you took is taking off." She smirked at them. "I posted it online."

"What?" Wallace peered down at the screen.

"What did you do?" Marco and Polo squeezed in to get a closer look. "Is that the RACCOONS?" Polo squealed. "They're so much clearer than on the TV!"

"But it's just the part where they eat the treats," Marco said. "Why'd you tape that?"

"Once the bigwigs at Beautiful Buffet Cat Food see that, I'm betting these raccoons will be the new face of those caviar cat treats," the white cat said smugly.

"But that's your job!" Butterbean said. "Aren't you the face of Beautiful Buffet Cat Food?"

"The cat food, sure," the white cat said. "I'm practically an institution. NOBODY is going to replace me there. But the treats campaign?" She rolled her eyes. "They can have it. Those raccoons really sell it. I mean, look at them—they're adorable!"

She took Reginald aside. "Seriously, this thing is going to be huge. I could make you all big stars."

Reginald laughed. "Thanks, but no thanks. I don't think any of us want that, right, guys?"

Tulip shook her head. "I just want to keep the tube top."

"Besides, there's a high rise three blocks over that looks promising," Reginald said. "It has a sushi restaurant on the first level."

"Sushi?" Chad slithered in from the kitchen, where he'd been helping himself to some tuna. "What's this I hear about sushi?"

"Don't even think about it, Chad," Oscar said. "You'd never make it that far on pavement. Think about your tentacles."

Chad flexed his tentacles defensively. "I do have sensitive skin."

"Well, if you ever change your mind, let me know," the white cat said, pouting. "You could be the most famous raccoons in town."

"I think they already are," Butterbean said.

"Oh, hey, Doc, that reminds me," Reginald said quietly. "I've got something here for that friend of yours. Hope it'll make things right between us. I washed it myself."

Butterbean examined Reginald's present. "Ooooh,

that'll be perfect," she said. "Thank you." She beamed up at him. "You were always my favorite patient."

"He was always your ONLY patient," Walt said in a low voice.

"Still," Butterbean said. "My favorite."

Reginald's nose turned pink. Then he cleared his throat. "Well, as fun as this is, we'd better get out of here before Animal Control shows up. Say your good-byes, everyone."

Tulip the raccoon lunged forward and grabbed Oscar in a strangle hug, and then went for Walt. Apparently the raccoons were big huggers. No one escaped unhugged.

"Yeah, we'd better get our stuff together and get back out to the loading dock too," Dunkin said. "Ken's got a shuffleboard championship to win."

Ken nodded solemnly.

"If you guys ever need anything, well, we're right outside. Right, Wallace?" He punched Wallace lightly on the arm.

"Right," Wallace said, rubbing his arm as he waved goodbye.

The apartment felt especially quiet after the raccoons and rats left. "Well, I guess that's it, then," Oscar said quietly.

"Not quite," Butterbean said. "There's still one thing that I have to do."

"Butterbean, nooo, not again!" Madison squealed as Butterbean dragged her off the elevator and down the hall of the second floor.

Butterbean jumped up and pawed at the door until Madison caught up.

"Fine!" Madison grumbled. "I can't believe you!" she said, knocking at the door. It wasn't like she had much choice, not since Butterbean had already body-slammed it.

Mrs. Biscuit opened the door a crack and peeked out. "Oh, it's you!" she said, opening the door wider. "Come on in. I know he'll be glad to see you."

"Well, it's ABOUT TIME," Biscuit barked, rushing over to Butterbean. "I've been DYING over here. Do you know how hard it is not to bark? I had to stuff my face into the couch cushions at least ten times a day! So what's the latest? Did you rip those raccoons to shreds?"

"Um, not quite," Butterbean said. "They were actually very nice. I don't know if you caught their performance earlier on the building surveillance channel?"

"I don't watch TV," Biscuit said snippily.

"Well, anyway, they were very good. And they're relocating, so you shouldn't have any more problems." She eyed Biscuit's bangs. "With the barking, that is."

"Did you tell them I'd pulverize them? Did they quake in their boots when they found out who they were up against? Is that why they ran away? Because I could TAKE THEM APART." Biscuit curled his lip in the most threatening way. (Unfortunately, it just looked like he had something caught in his teeth.)

"No, but the raccoon leader did send you a gift." Butterbean shook vigorously, and Reginald's gift fell down from where Polo had tucked it underneath her collar. "His name is Reginald."

Biscuit nosed it carefully. Then he looked up, his lip quivering. "Are those? I mean . . ."

"They're barrettes," Butterbean said. "He thought they'd be a good look."

Biscuit picked up the barrettes and rushed over to Mrs. Biscuit, flinging them violently into her lap.

"Oh, did you bring a gift?" She looked up at Madison quizzically.

Madison looked over at Butterbean, who wagged her tail.

"I mean . . . yes?" Madison said. Sometimes it was better just to go with it.

"These are perfect!" Mrs. Biscuit held the barrettes up to look at them. "They're beautiful!" She leaned forward and whispered to Madison so Biscuit couldn't hear. "I don't know if you can tell, but he had a little mishap at the groomer. I think it's been getting him down. These will do just the trick."

"Oh really? I hadn't noticed," Madison lied. She had totally noticed.

Mrs. Biscuit bent down and snapped the barrettes into place, transforming Biscuit's heavy bangs into two jaunty ponytails.

"Perfect!" Mrs. Biscuit said, clapping her hands together.

Biscuit raced over to the window and peered at his reflection. When he turned back, his eyes were moist. "Butterbean, that raccoon . . ." He sniffed loudly. "I can't even . . ." He swallowed hard. "You guys are the best."

— 20 —

"WELL?" MRS. FOOD LOOKED UP AS MADISON and Butterbean came into the apartment. "How did it go? Is Butterbean going to be a therapy dog?" She muted the Television program she'd been watching.

"How did it go? Terrible, that's how it went," Madison said, unclipping Butterbean's leash and throwing herself into a chair.

"I failed!" Butterbean said cheerfully, trotting over to Oscar's cage.

"Oh no!" Oscar said, hopping to the end of his perch. "I'm sorry, Bean."

"Oh no!" Mrs. Food said sympathetically. "What happened?"

"They just didn't appreciate my techniques," Butterbean said with a shrug.

"What didn't happen?" Madison grumbled. "She did EVERYTHING wrong."

Mrs. Food chuckled. "I'm sure it wasn't that bad."

"Oh, it was," Butterbean said.

Madison started counting on her fingers. "One, she jumped up on everyone in the room and licked them in the face, no matter how many times I tried to get her to stop. And not just once. Repeatedly."

"They weren't very friendly," Butterbean said. "I tried to win them over, but it didn't work."

"Two, she refused to sit and stay when I told her to," Madison went on. "It's like she'd never heard the words before!"

Oscar raised an eyebrow. "But you know how to sit and stay."

"They brought another dog in!" Butterbean said defensively. "OF COURSE I had to go say hello. I was just being POLITE." Butterbean pouted. "I don't see why they would hold that against me."

"Three, she ate the food that they put out, even after I told her to leave it," Madison said. "I told her a million times!"

"It was ON THE FLOOR!" Butterbean said indignantly. "It's not like it BELONGED to anyone."

"But it was a test!" Oscar pointed out. "You were supposed to leave it alone."

"I didn't want it to go to waste," Butterbean said. "It was PERFECTLY GOOD FOOD."

"It's not your fault," Walt said, inspecting her tail. "It sounds like it was a setup."

"Do I need to go on?" Madison said, throwing up her hands. "Everything she did was wrong."

"Poor Madison," Mrs. Food said. "After you tried so hard."

"They didn't even have a couch," Butterbean grumbled, lying down. "I didn't even find out about their childhoods. It wasn't what I think of as therapy at all."

"It's okay, Butterbean. Maybe you weren't meant to be a therapy dog," Polo said sympathetically.

"Yeah, if they won't even let you eat loose food," Marco agreed. "What good is it?"

"It's fine. I'm thinking of opening a private practice," Butterbean said thoughtfully. "Maybe keep it small at first . . . it's just an idea." She looked up hopefully. "Do you think Reginald and Biscuit would be willing to give me references?"

Walt sighed and looked at Oscar, who shrugged. "Sure. Why not."

Mrs. Food patted Madison on the leg. "Well, that's too bad. I'm sure they'll let you try again," she said.

"Nope, I think I'm just done. I'll just—OH!" Madison sat up. "Look, on the TV—aren't those the raccoons from the surveillance channel?"

Mrs. Food frowned and unmuted the Television. "I mean, they're raccoons, but . . ."

Madison pointed at the screen. "See? The way that raccoon is holding the treats bag—I'm sure it's the group that was in our storage room!"

Mrs. Food leaned forward. "No, I don't think so, Madison," she said after a few seconds. "These raccoons are obviously trained professionals. They've got music and costumes. And the video is much clearer." Then she laughed. "Besides, nobody was filming our raccoons, and that's hardly footage from the surveillance camera."

Madison grinned. "Right. It's not like there was a cameraman down there."

"Exactly." Mrs. Food smiled.

"Um," Wallace raised a hand. "Hello? I'm RIGHT HERE."

"I can't believe the white cat was right. They ARE famous," Oscar said, shaking his head.

"I can't believe it's on the Television so fast!" Butterbean said.

"I can't believe they're using raccoons to sell those treats," Walt scoffed. "It's like they're admitting cats won't eat them."

Mrs. Food looked down at Walt thoughtfully. "Hmm. Maybe Walt would like those treats? The raccoons really seem to enjoy them."

Walt gagged involuntarily.

Madison picked her up and petted her head. "I don't know. Don't forget that those are actor raccoons," she said. "Who knows what the treats really taste like?"

"Thank you. Exactly," Walt said, her stomach recovering. "Don't ever mention those treats to me again."

"Oh, look at how late it is!" Mrs. Food turned off the Television. "Madison, go get your coat. Carmen is back in town, and I told her we'd meet her to see a movie this afternoon. Sound good?"

Madison put Walt down quickly. "Sure!

"She wants to hear about all the weirdness from this week," Mrs. Food said, going to the door and picking up her jacket.

"Oh! Talking about weird!" Madison said, putting on her shoes. "I forgot to tell you. I ran into that woman in the elevator this morning. You know, the one on seven?" Madison said.

"You're going to have to be more specific," Mrs. Food said dryly.

"The one who power walks?" Madison said. "That lady?"

"Oh right, I know who you're talking about." Mrs. Food nodded.

"Mrs. Power Walker?" Butterbean's ears pricked up. "They're talking about Mrs. Power Walker!"

"Did you know she designs doll clothes? It's like, her job. And she said the weirdest thing." Madison put on her jacket. "She told me all that out of the blue, and then she said she hoped the clothes had been useful. Isn't that weird? What's that supposed to mean?"

"WHAT?" Marco and Polo looked at Wallace, whose eyes were wide.

Mrs. Food frowned. "That is strange. Useful how?"

"That's just it—I don't know," Madison said.

"I PUT THEM BACK!" Wallace said, looking around in disbelief. "HOW DID SHE KNOW?"

"She's just eccentric, I think," Mrs. Food said, picking up her keys. "If you see her again, just humor her and tell her how helpful they were."

"Did you hear that?" Butterbean barked, as Mrs. Food and Madison headed out the door. "They were talking about Mrs. Power Walker!"

"You bet I did," the white cat said, coming out from behind the couch. "She said the raccoons were OBVIOUSLY PROFESSIONAL! Somebody has good taste."

"Were you there the whole time?" Polo gasped. "YOU CAN'T DO THAT."

"Doesn't bother me," Chad said, climbing out of the sink in the kitchen.

"CHAD?" Marco said, whipping his head around. "YOU GUYS!"

"It sounds like she didn't mind you using the clothes," Walt said thoughtfully. "You know what this means, right, Wallace?" Walt said.

"You bet. Tiny clothes for everybody!" Wallace cheered. He'd really liked the little sailor shirt.

Walt shook her head. "Well, no, I was thinking—"

"Spy disguises for everybody!" Polo cheered.

"No, I was going to say—" Walt started again.

"Free snacks?" Butterbean said.

"Snacks?" Chad's voice came from the kitchen. It sounded like his mouth was full.

"It means things will finally be back to normal?" Oscar said wistfully. He was hoping to be retired again very soon. He still had that to-do list to tackle.

"You're all being ridiculous," the white cat sniffed. "That's not what it means."

"Thank you," Walt said. "I was going to say, it sounds like you've got your old roommate back, if you're still interested."

Wallace nodded, his eyes shining. "I can move back in!" He'd really missed living in Apartment 7C.

The white cat sniffed. "Well sure, I guess that could

be what it means. But you know what it *really* means?" A strange smile spread across her face.

"I don't even want to ask," Walt said. She didn't like that look.

"I'll ask!" Butterbean said, scooting forward in anticipation. "What does it really mean?"

"One word," the white cat said, a gleam in her eye. "COSTUMES!"

"Oh no." Oscar put his head under his wing.

"Oh yes," the white cat said, striking a pose. "That's right. It's SHOWTIME."

Acknowledgments

If you've ever seen a video of raccoons stealing cat food or washing their hands, you'll know where I got the idea for this book. So thanks to all the raccoon video stars out there and to the people who filmed them.

This book wouldn't have been possible without so many people. So huge thanks go out to:

Reka Simonsen (editor extraordinaire), Kate Testerman (agent extraordinaire), and Dave Mottram (artist extraordinaire); and to Kristie Choi, Michael McCartney, Clare McGlade, Tatyana Rosalia, Brian D. Luster, and everyone at Atheneum Books for Young Readers. You're all incredible.

My family, for reading endless drafts, and for being there for me to lean on. (So much leaning this year.)

The real-life Ken, for letting me borrow your name and turn you into a rodent shuffleboard champion.

Howdy, for putting down the red squeaky ball when I needed to concentrate (at least most of the time).

Everyone who reads my books. Seriously, you're awesome. (This means you. Yes, you.)

Special thanks also to:

Dr. Kaitlyn Beisecker-Levin, Dr. John Jane, Jr., Dr. Spencer Payne, Dr. Ashok Asthagiri, Dr. Gregory Hong, Dr. Nancy Vilar, Dr. Trae Robison, Dr. Connor Berlin, Dr. Kathryn Kearns, Dr. Delaney Carpenter, Dr. Ryan Kellogg, Dr. Panagiotis Mastorakos, Cassandra Freed-Pastor, Dawn Shaver, and everyone at the UVA Neurosurgery department for all your help. I honestly can't thank you enough.

The nurses at UVA 6 West. You were all so wonderful. I can't tell you how much I appreciate it.

And finally, for providing pandemic distractions (still!), thanks to everyone behind *Wordle*, *Worldle*, *Squareword*, *Statele*, *Heardle*, and any other "le" games I missed. (I'm pretty sure I played them all.)

Turn the page for a sneak peek at
THE GREAT CATNAPPING

"Butterbean, don't move!" Walt peered down from her perch on top of the bookshelf. There was an intruder in the apartment, and it was slowly making its way across the living room. Toward Butterbean.

Walt's eyes widened. "It's right behind you!"

Butterbean tried not to move. But the words "it's right behind you" made that impossible. She let out an earsplitting squeal and propelled herself out from under the coffee table and up onto the back of the couch.

"I said DON'T move," Walt hissed as she watched Butterbean scramble to keep her footing.

"My tail was exposed!" Butterbean wailed. She'd

gotten too big to fit under the coffee table anymore, but it was still her go-to hiding spot. "I'm attached to my tail!"

The intruder didn't seem to have noticed Butterbean or her tail. It passed by the coffee table (right where Butterbean's tail had been) and hesitated briefly. Then it turned and disappeared into the kitchen.

Walt sighed in relief. "All clear." She shook her head. "We can't keep hiding forever. We have to do something."

"Mrs. Food wouldn't have brought it here if it was dangerous," Oscar said from his birdcage. "I think we should confront it. Head on. Be brave." He puffed up his feathers. Oscar was a mynah bird, so he was already pretty big, but it never hurt to puff up. It was easier to be brave when he looked bigger.

"Easy for you to say," Walt snorted. "You're not a cat. You're safe in your cage."

"True," Oscar admitted. "But I'm still not convinced it's a threat."

Walt growled in frustration. She'd had plans for the day. Big plans. And those plans hadn't included hiding out on top of a bookshelf all afternoon. Maybe Oscar was right—Mrs. Food wouldn't intentionally bring doom on the entire apartment. But everyone makes mistakes, Mrs. Food included. And that thing in the kitchen looked like a big mistake.

"Well, we've got to do SOMETHING," Polo said from the rat cage. "Wallace is coming over later, and I don't know if one wild rat would be able to win a fight with that thing."

"Plus he's technically a GUEST," Marco said from the food dish. "It's rude to let your guests get eaten."

Wallace was their rat friend from the vents (and occasional roommate). He was currently living in Apartment 7C with Mrs. Power Walker. (She didn't realize that, though.) He spent a lot of time visiting Mrs. Food's apartment. (She didn't realize that either.)

"Wallace is pretty strong, though," Marco said thoughtfully. "He might win. He's almost as strong as me."

"Yeah, but the intruder is a lot bigger than Wallace," Polo said.

"Well, maybe, but we can't keep hiding forever," Marco said, throwing up his arms. "We're virtual PRISONERS."

"Can't keep hiding from what?" The white cat stalked out from behind the sofa and sat down in the living room. She was another resident of the Strathmore Building that stopped by Mrs. Food's apartment periodically, almost always without an invitation. (Mrs. Food didn't know about that either.)

"CAT! TAKE COVER!" Butterbean yelped from

her spot on the couch cushions. "There's a THING in the apartment!"

The white cat raised an eyebrow. "Really? A thing?" She sniffed. "Ooooh, I'm SOO SCARED." She didn't look scared.

"Laugh if you want, but it'll be back any second," Walt said.

"It's like it's patrolling," Oscar agreed. "We're going to confront it when it gets back from the kitchen."

"The kitchen, huh? I'll just take a quick peek," the white cat said, standing up and fluffing her fur.

"NOOO!" Butterbean yelped. "You can't just—" But the white cat was gone before she even finished the sentence.

"Well, so much for the white cat," Walt said gloomily. "She's doomed."

"It's too bad. She was a nice cat," Polo said, sighing.

Marco shot her a skeptical look.

"Okay, she was a cat that didn't eat us. Better?" Polo said.

"Better," Marco said. Accuracy was important to him.

Polo put her hands over her ears. "Let me know when the screaming stops."

The animals all braced themselves. But there was no screaming.

"Do you think it got her?" Marco said after a minute. "Mrs. Food isn't going to like finding a body in her kitchen."

"Shh," Oscar said. "I think it's coming back." The animals all turned toward the kitchen, just in time to see the intruder glide into the room. With the white cat on its back.

"But . . . How . . ." Butterbean said, losing her footing and slipping in between two of the cushions.

"You guys are ridiculous," the white cat said, extending one paw and licking it casually. "You know that, right?"

Butterbean's eyes widened. "But what did you DO? Did you TAME IT?"

"I didn't DO anything," the white cat said. "I didn't have to, because . . ."

The door to Mrs. Food's office opened down the hall.

"HIDE!" Walt screeched.

"Oops." The white cat's eyes widened. In one graceful motion, she stood up and jumped off the intruder's back, ducking quickly behind the sofa.

Mrs. Food appeared in the hallway, took one look at the assembled pets, and laughed. "Look at you. You're all so silly. I told you! It's perfectly safe."

"First we're ridiculous and now we're silly," Oscar said with a sour expression. "Noted."

"So our safety is a big joke to her," Walt muttered under her breath.

"I don't feel like laughing," Butterbean said, trying to get a better footing on the couch cushions. Apparently they weren't meant to support a small wiener dog.

"I told you. It's just a vacuum cleaner!" Mrs. Food said, her hands on her hips. "Look." She turned to open the door to the hall closet. "It's just like this one! But smaller." She moved the coats aside to reveal a heavy push-style vacuum cleaner.

Butterbean squealed again and shrank back, her feet flailing against the cushions. "Is that supposed to make it BETTER? That closet thing is TERRIFYING!"

"So loud," Marco said solemnly. He was eating a sunflower seed and had his feet up. He was pretty sure there was no way either one of those vacuum cleaners could squeeze into a rat cage.

"Very scary," Polo agreed from the top of the water bottle. "I've never liked it. So much screaming."

"Although to be fair, the screaming comes from Butterbean and not the vacuum," Oscar said. He didn't love the vacuum either, but he didn't make a big production of it. Not like Butterbean. Butterbean had to be banished to the office whenever it was vacuuming day.

"You'll get used to it, I promise," Mrs. Food said. "Before too long, you'll be thanking your lucky stars that I won it in that raffle. Look, it's so quiet! So unobtrusive!" The small vacuum cleaner bounced against the stand to Oscar's cage, almost knocking it over before swiveling and heading off into the dining room.

"Agree to disagree," Oscar said, clicking his beak doubtfully.

Muffled snickers came from behind the couch.

"Well, it's much quieter anyway. And that's a definite improvement. Right, Butterbean?" Mrs. Food shot Butterbean a significant look as she turned and went into the kitchen.

Butterbean tried to look dignified, but the couch cushions were sucking her down fast. "I can't help the screaming," she muttered finally as the cushion collapsed under her weight.

The snickers behind the couch got even louder.

"Why are you even here?" Butterbean said grouchily to the white cat. "You're not supposed to be here when Mrs. Food's out and about."

"Oh, I have some news that I think Walt will find particularly interesting." The white cat poked her head out from behind the couch and winked.

Walt groaned. "Why do I think I'm not going to want to hear this?" she sighed. "Spill it."

The white cat's eyes gleamed. "You'll find out. I just want to be here when you do."

"Look, cat—" Walt started. But she was interrupted by the sound of the door slamming open. Madison Park, the medium-sized girl who lived with Mrs. Food, hurried inside. (Madison had never learned the art of quiet door opening.)

"Mrs. Fudeker! Guess what?" she said, dumping her book bag onto the floor in a heap. "You'll never believe it."

"Here we go," the white cat said smugly.

"What won't I believe?" Mrs. Food came out of the kitchen. "Watch out for the new vacuum," she said as it glided toward Madison.

"Oh cool, you won? That's awesome!" The raffle had been the big excitement of the week. Madison had been secretly hoping they'd win the entertainment system, but the robot vacuum was good too. She stepped to the side and watched as the vacuum bumped into her book bag and turned around. "It's so quiet!"

"Isn't it?" Mrs. Food said, shooting another pointed look at Butterbean. "Now, what's your news?"

"The news is, I got a JOB!" Madison folded her arms proudly. "A real one!"

"I thought we were her job," Butterbean pouted.

"Shh, Butterbean. We're not a job anymore. Now we're family," Oscar said.

"But what—" Mrs. Food started, but Madison interrupted.

"You know that white cat on the fifth floor? The famous one?" Madison said, bobbing up and down on the balls of her feet with excitement.

"I love this kid," the white cat said from behind the couch.

"Right, the one in the commercials," Mrs. Food said. "Are you going to be a pet sitter again?"

Madison shook her head. "No, this is way better! I'm going to be a cat wrangler!"

Mrs. Food looked confused.

"It's a kind of cat assistant," Madison explained. "You know that supermarket that they're opening down the street? They're going to have a big grand opening tomorrow and the white cat is going to make a celebrity appearance. And they hired me to help out! Bob recommended me. Isn't that great?"

"That's incredible!" Mrs. Food clapped her hands together. "That's so nice of Bob. I hope you thanked him."

"Don't worry, I did," Madison said. Bob was the maintenance man in the Strathmore Building. He pretty much ran everything there.

Mrs. Food looked at Madison proudly. "Well, congratulations, you'll be perfect."

"You're doing a supermarket opening?" Oscar said, shooting a look at the couch.

The white cat's eyes were barely visible in the shadows. They narrowed. "Did you not hear her? It's a CELEBRITY appearance. I'm the CELEBRITY."

"Supermarket opening," Walt snickered. "Well, that's great for you. You wouldn't catch me dead at one of those things. But whatever floats your boat."

"Funny you should say that," the white cat smirked.

"And I haven't even told you the best part!" Madison said, bobbing up and down even faster. "It's not just me they want!"

Mrs. Food looked doubtful. "They want me too? I don't know, Madison. I've got bridge club tomorrow. Besides, I'm not sure I'm up for working a supermarket grand opening."

Madison laughed. "No, not you! And it's okay if you say no, but they want to have another cat at the opening. A regular cat."

"Oh no." Walt felt like she'd turned to stone.

"Wait, do you mean—" Mrs. Food's eyes widened.

"That's right, WALT!" Madison cheered. "She's going to be a STAR!"

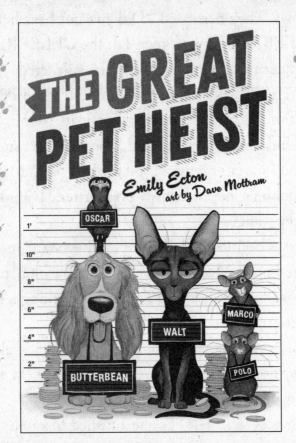